THE
HAUNTED NORTH

*Paranormal tales from Aberdeen
and the North East*

By

Graeme Milne

Published by

Cauliay Publishing & Distribution
PO Box 12076
Aberdeen
AB16 9AL
www.cauliaypublishing.com

First Edition

ISBN 978-0-9558992-1-8
Copyright © Graeme Milne 2008

Cover design. Cauliay Publishing

Dedication

Dedicated to my parents Alan and Geraldine, for always being there, I could not have asked for better. To Sandra Stewart for wise words and laughs in the face of adversity and an especially huge thank you to Carol for her for love and support, for being a source of inspiration, for being patient, but most of all for being my best friend.

Acknowledgements

Duncan Haig, Sandy, Eileen, Raymond and all at Provost Skenes House, Chris Begg, Thane Lawrie, Derek Pyper, Craig, Frank and Pete at the Moorings, Jean.Horne, Mike at the former ministry, Heather, Geoff, Helen, First Bus Aberdeen, Aberdeen City Library services, Aberdeen City Archives, Aberdeen Central Library, Local Studies Department, Aberdeen City Council Archaeology Unit, Michael Molden, Melissa Rossi, staff at Powis Community Centre, Adele, Aberdeen Foyer, Stanley Robertson, Annie Mcintosh, Eileen and Michael Davies, Maryland Library Archive, Karen London, Jim Mcdonald, Staff at Kaimhill community centre, Mike, John Smilie, Colin and Jean Muir, Kenny Luke, Diane Bowman, Rob, Annie Scott, Helen, Ashgrove Family Centre, Anne Garden, Fiona, Sally, Fiona Clark, lil, Francis, Ian Esslemont, Ben, Valerie and Terry Wright, Dorothy, Jim, Mike, Eileen, Sheila, Rob, Sandra, Connie, Chris and also my family and friends for their encouragement and kind words. And lastly, a special thanks to all who have assisted in providing support during this project, without your help it would never have happened!

Contents

Introduction

Ghosts or spirits as I prefer to call them are everywhere in grand palatial mansions, pubs, theatres, in your home and mine, in fact anywhere that people have lived and died, or at the very least spent some time in. I personally believe that spirit exists in a parallel world to ours and under the right circumstances, when the 'veil is lifted', they can manifest themselves. I must point out however, that ghosts and spirits to me are entirely different in both their existence and purpose, and I feel it is important to try and understand the fundamental difference. I look on ghosts as none sentient replays from the past that appear to follow set patterns of behaviour, while spirits are as alive as we are albeit on a higher realm of existence. Though spirit can manifest itself on our physical plain, it requires effort beyond our comprehension, and so we must be satisfied with the tantalizing glimpses we are offered when our worlds cross.

When researching for this book I asked myself: "What usually disappoints me when reading about the paranormal?" The answer is twofold, firstly a lack of background information on the alleged locations and secondly the blind acceptance of many of our most durable tales which being oft repeated have been embellished to the point of fantasy. Many people believe the accumulative experiences of those who have lived in a location adds to a buildings history and spiritual make up leaving residual energy or imprint of events from the past. How many times have you entered a building and thought it had a nice atmosphere or indeed a 'bad vibe' it can certainly play a huge part when choosing a home. It is natural to assume that the older the building the greater chance of activity due to the layers of emotion that have built up, though there are exceptions.

Having read many 'ghost books' over the years, I certainly had a passing interest in the subject, however I could honestly say I have no recollection of anything paranormal invading my life at that time. An incident occurred not long after my 21st birthday which though not life changing certainly caused me to be more open minded. I was invited by a girlfriend to stay overnight in Edinburgh, which I accepted. Things went rapidly downhill upon my arrival as she had omitted to tell her parents that I was staying overnight. The situation caused much embarrassment all round. Her father, having just bought a property on the edge of Dunfermline, and temporarily staying in a hotel had no provision for guests and made it quite clear that he was unhappy with the situation. Being the innocent party in all this, I naively thought they would let me sleep on a chair, but alas, no. After much discussion it was decided that I could spend the night in their new home, and so I was driven to Dunfermline. The house itself was situated in a quiet street, a former Victorian manse it looked forbidding. I was filled with apprehension, a feeling that was amplified as I was shown where I was to sleep. I was taken to a large room off the downstairs hall, given a sleeping bag, pillow, and was wished a goodnight before they headed back to the discomfort of their four star hotel. The room I was in was not pitch black due to a streetlight at the end of the front garden, but it was very quiet and as you can imagine every creak and groan from the woodwork was magnified. The room was devoid of furniture not even a chair, so I went into my sleeping bag and lay down, resting my head against the wall. I must have eventually fallen asleep though I lay awake listening to my heart thumping in my chest for what seemed ages. I still have no idea how long I had been asleep; all I know is that I felt the bottom of the sleeping bag being tugged sharply and my head cracking on the wooden floor. I was wide awake in a split second, scared, and lying a good two feet from the wall. I got up and lit a cigarette, one of many to follow and spent the rest of the night sitting upright, watching the room getting lighter as dawn approached. The sleeping bag on the wooden floor could have caused me to move as I slept, I rationalised, but it did not explain the fact that I felt pulled along the floor and that I ended up so far from the wall. After a long wait the sun began to appear and eventually I was picked up by her family, I don't remember what I did that day or indeed if I told anyone about my experience it has all blurred with time but I still remember that night with great clarity.

Though the incident was perplexing it wasn't till my mothers passing, some years later, and her subsequent visitation that I began to seriously question everything, sparking an interest in spiritualism and the mysteries of the afterlife. At a very unhappy time in my life I felt, retrospectively, that the following events were meant to offer me comfort, but at the time, I am ashamed to say caused me great alarm. A student at the time, I was living in a dilapidated tenement in Union Grove, Aberdeen. I had gone to bed, under the influence of nothing stronger than a cup of tea I might add, and was soon fast asleep having left the light on. I must have subconsciously been aware of someone standing at the foot of the bed as I awoke with an almighty shout, sat bolt upright in time to see a misty, grey, human shaped form. The strangest thing then occurred, which is as clear today as it was over twelve years ago. As I sat up in bed I witnessed the mist being sucked into what I can only describe as a void, looking like a smoke machine working in reverse. My heart was pounding and I was in a state of alarm and in the confusion my eyes were drawn to the clock on my bedside table, it was at three, the significance of this time would become apparent later. I can't remember if I fell asleep again that night.

Around a week later I spoke to my dad about my experiences, his eyes widened, then, he told me an almost identical story which had took place the day after my own experience, strangely, also at three in the morning. He also awoke with a shout seeing a figure at the foot of the bed, but this time the figure went out the door, which was ajar. It was not long after, out of curiosity, that I went to see a medium who stated that my mother had come to comfort me, but left as she was aware that I was afraid. As previously mentioned I felt terribly guilty about my reaction. The medium then went on to describe in accurate detail my family, gave relevant names and also described the kind of paintings I had been working on at college. My mum had apparently been watching me and passed on detailed information to the medium about the kind of colours I had been using, which amazed me.

Years passed and I developed a keen interest in the subject, enrolling in awareness classes at a local spiritualist centre. Each session would start with a meditation to calm the mind, usually followed by a talk on the history of the spiritualist movement, occasionally taking part in demonstrations. These were usually nerve-wracking affairs but also exciting and thought provoking. It was during my two years at the centre that I became aware of the different gifts mediums are given when working for spirit, clairvoyance, the ability to see, clairaudience, the ability to hear and clairsentience, the ability to pick up feelings and emotions. My own sensitivity began to develop during this period and I found that I was able to walk into certain buildings and pick up on cold spots, feelings and occasionally get information in the form of images. I started to look at the possibility of writing a book though I did not want to try and 'convert' anyone but rather try and provide evidence that could be appreciated by all and at least provide food for thought. Concentrating my research in Aberdeen has proved interesting, particularly as it is my home town, though I have forayed out into the shire on occasion if the story was to interesting to ignore. Many of the locations you will find have never been investigated before and others though documented, have, I think been added to, providing a fuller picture. Deciding to come at the subject from a more spiritualist point of view, rather than the usual 'Halloween ghost in a white sheet scenario', I feel has added a different dimension, if you will forgive the pun. It is has also been a surprise, though a pleasant one to me, how willing people have been to share their experiences and of the sheer diversity of incidents. I must, however, stress at this point, that I am not a practising medium, rather, I have relied on my sensitivity to 'pick up' on what I consider to be communication and have relied on my dogged determination to try and separate fact from fiction. Most experiences, I have found, are of a benign nature though at other times there is mischief and on occasion something darker, a possible reflection of personality and circumstance.

You will read about the benign spirit that still resides in the rooms of Provost Skenes House, Guestrow. A plethora of activity in the Moorings bar located near Aberdeen's drowning pool, the 'Pottie', and the elusive Captain Beaton at First Bus, who still makes his presence felt among staff, among a host of others. If you believe that we retain our personality in the next life, then it is only natural to assume that not everyone we meet is going to be a well rounded human being. You could argue that this might be due to an accumulation of unhappy experiences imprinted on a place, rather than any one individual. It is also worth pointing out, that spirit activity takes many forms and it is rare to find completely earthbound spirits. In most cases it could be classed as a residual energy, however, I do believe that many spirit people enjoy interacting with us and are interested in what is going on around them, hence are happy to let their presence be felt. On a final note, as in all good mysteries, we are, as you would expect, left with far more questions than answers.

The Moorings

The Moorings bar is situated on Trinity Quay, Aberdeen and has historically been linked to spirit merchants—the alcohol variety—since the 16th or 17th century when an alleged coaching house stood on the site. The main thoroughfare into Aberdeen and to the north at that time ran from the Hardgate, one of Aberdeen's most ancient roads, along the harbour front before heading out of the city. It is perfectly feasible that an inn would have stood in the vicinity due to the number of coaches using this route and in modern terms would have been situated in a prime location. The harbour as we know it undoubtedly looked entirely different and was unable to accommodate large vessels.

In the 16th century the harbour was little more than a shallow natural basin. Still to be dredged it had many natural obstacles to overcome, the sand banks which would be exposed at low tide and the rocks proving hazardous to larger vessels. One such rock was known as Knock Maitland. It was and was described as being an 'immense boulder', eventually removed in 1610 it did much to improve the burgeoning harbour. During this period smaller vessels were employed to ferry goods from those ships, unable to navigate the shallow channel to the dockside. These large ships were forced to drop anchor in Aberdeen bay being at the mercy of the weather and running the risk of pirate attack. Aberdeen harbour at that time was not only used for the transportation of goods but also used as a means of execution with its 'drowning pool' used six times between 1584 and 1587 for the crime of murder and infanticide. During those years it was recorded that a number of men and women were publicly drowned by having their hands and feet bound before being unceremoniously thrown into the icy waters. The drowning pool known locally as the 'Pottie' was situated in close proximity to the present day Moorings Bar at Shore Brae and was certainly not an uncommon punishment at that time in Scotland. It was a practice which was to be continued in the persecution of 'witches'. It was also noted that in 1582 a crane was erected in the vicinity with the express purpose of 'ducking' miscreants.

The earliest records of the current building I could find date from 1841 although in earlier maps of Aberdeen other buildings are clearly shown. I could find no record as to what they were used for though it is intriguing to speculate that it could perhaps be the aforementioned coaching inn. In the 1854-55 post office directory a number of people lived there including coal brokers, paper manufacturers and nearby a number of vintners, wine sellers or wine makers which must have been a popular occupation due to their prolific numbers in the area. The first owner of the establishment was Simon McLeod, born on the 28th of August in 1857 at James Street in Aberdeen. The son of a grocer, his name appears in the 1881 census as resident of 2 Trinity Quay where his widowed mother Isabella was one of the many spirit merchants in the area. The bar became known as Simon McLeod's and remained so for many years though Simon himself appears to have either sold or leased the pub to a number of people from 1911 onwards with spirit dealers John Mackie and Frederick Glegg being mentioned in directories of the time. Simon himself died in1949 living to the ripe old age of 91 at 7 Queens Road in what would I assume be more comfortable surroundings than Trinity Quay, which had at that time of his youth a reputation as being 'rough'. The name stuck and so remained until 1965 when the name the "Moorings" first appears in the Aberdeen directory and thus remains to this day with the current owner being only the third person to do so in the last forty years. I first met current owner Craig 'Flash' Adams after following up an enquiry as to the authenticity of ghost stories I had heard. Regulars had mentioned for years the fact that the bar was supposed to be haunted and that certain areas of the premises had an 'atmosphere'.

I am always aware that following up 'stories' can result in a dead end, no pun intended or in the worse case scenario, scorn, but was pleasantly surprised to find that Craig along with other staff members were more than willing to share their experiences. It appeared he was just as curious as I was about the incidents and how they had been affecting the running of the bar. In keeping with the traditional clichés associated with the ghost story, the weather on the night of the meeting turned out to be inclement. This was an understatement, and when I arrived, sat dripping, pondering on what would be the outcome of the evening. I met with Craig and was taken down to the cellars to have a look round and was told that when he became the new owner in 2002 there were already rumours circulating among regulars about the strange goings on particularly in one cellar area. The cellar floor had been cemented over fairly recently but was initially cobbled as were most of the other buildings in the street, though this did not detract from the palpable atmosphere in the room. It appeared on the face of it to be much older than the top part of the building and in amongst the many interesting nooks and crannies were the remains of an ancient stone fireplace still visible despite the present whitewash. We proceeded to the taproom. The nerve centre of the bar is housed behind a modern chipboard wall and it was there I was told that who ever was at large in the basement, enjoyed tampering with the taps, frequently turning them off. This I was told goes through periods of happening regularly with staff having to make the trip down to the cellar to change barrels only to find they were still full. Though it has become a nuisance to staff it is seen as a practical joke rather than anything to malicious. I met barman Pete, who verified this by stating that it causes him much annoyance not to mention a certain amount of unease. Craig, in turn demonstrated that to turn the taps off takes a considerable amount of effort. Being unable to offer no rational explanation as to why the equipment could do this without someone's intervention, we left the area.

The atmosphere in the cellar is certainly not a light one and I must admit I had the distinct impression of being watched as if someone was curious about our activities. The thing that struck me most whilst I was there was the lack of noise from clientele in the upstairs bar, with the loud music, which plays continually being reduced in the cellar to a series of muffled, barely audible noises. There was something strange about being close to all the activity in the bar and still feeling isolated and was told that on a number of occasions the owner had ran up the stairs after nerves had got the better of him. To add to the desolate surroundings the cellar has flooded a number of times due to exceptionally high tides as have many others in the area leaving a clearly visible water mark on the walls. We continued our tour and I was then taken to the storage room where Craig completes his paperwork at night, an area he doesn't enjoy working in. Given the solitude of the room and having the only furniture in the cellar it is the most practical location to do this though given what he told me next, I would not relish the prospect of being alone there. It was in this room that two of the most frightening experiences took place, which he has never forgotten. My attention was drawn to an old price list on the wall and it was the removal of the list that inadvertently caused upset to one of the spirit visitors though more of that in a moment. Objects in the bar were being inexplicably moved especially after closing time when the bar was being cleaned up. These included a knife being flipped from the bar as if thrown. As if this wasn't enough, other incidents began to take place. A mop bucket on wheels was moved across the floor by invisible hands and there was also talk of people being shoved near the toilet doors and the sensation of being watched. After these incidents and much discussion they came to the conclusion that they might actually have a ghost, and if so who was it?

Ted a former Canadian airman had worked for a previous owner, helping round the bar and doing cellar work. He was popular with everyone, liked playing jokes and when he passed over was much missed, but had he left completely? It would seem that this was not the case. Ted had been seen a number of times either in the cellar or bizarrely in the space between the inner and outer toilet doors which may explain why there had been many reports of people being 'tripped' in that area. He had been seen 'appearing to work' in the cellar near an old wooden staircase that leads up to street level and where beer kegs would have been delivered. This I reasoned might not be as unusual as it seems for it is believed that certain spirit people like to engage in the tasks they did in the physical life and return to familiar surroundings. It is not without substance either to suggest that the witness may have been picking up on residual energy, a recording of Ted and his activities rather than an interactive visitation due to their own sensitivity. This though would not explain the objects being moved. Another theory is that perhaps there is more than one spirit active in the bar, a theory given credence when Craig decided to conduct an experiment. As previously mentioned an old price list hangs in the downstairs office, the prices and type beers on offer suggested it was from the 1970s. Craig had decided to clear up some of the bits and pieces that had accumulated downstairs and removed the list among other items from the area. Coincidentally he had mulled over the idea of placing recording equipment in the cellar and leave it running all night to see if anything unusual could be picked up. He was interested in the concept of EVP, (electronic voice phenomena) where spirit noises or, voices can sometimes be recorded onto tape, if left running in an active location. It is usually a laborious task with researchers having to listen to hours of white noise in the hope of capturing something and is by no means a definitive indication of a haunting due to external noise from traffic, passers by or in most cases buildings naturally settling at night. A few nights later he moved the recording equipment and speakers into the cellar and along with microphones locked the area down for the night. The next day he began the onerous task of sifting through the recordings and spent some time listening to white noise before a voice boomed out appearing to say: "put the price list back", which caused him great alarm as it could clearly be heard through the headphones. He continued to replay the recording and became convinced that message was as he had thought. He surmised that the voice could have belonged to a previous owner/worker though proving this would be nigh on impossible. The voice was also heard by barman Frank, who was present when the recording was played back. He stated that the equipment used was up to date and unlikely to cause sound abnormalities. Frank also became the recipient of some unexplained phenomena when he stated:

15

"A door was pushed against me, when there was no one else in the building," and was witness to chairs being moved under the same circumstances. He also witnessed "what seemed like smoke or steam appearing for no apparent reason and dissipating quickly". He pointed out that although some people "get freaked out" by these incidents he felt relaxed about it all.

Perhaps the most frightening incident occurred in the late spring of 2005. Craig had been approached by the police, days before the incident, who were trying to trace the whereabouts of a missing person. Craig knew Jane (real name omitted) well enough having been a regular for some time and had not seen her recently. she unfortunately had an alcohol problem and was well known by everyone at the bar. He admitted that he soon put the visit to the back of his mind and carried on with the business of running his establishment. A few days later he was in his office having locked up and was absorbed in the usual paperwork when something fluttered down from the ceiling and landed onto his desk. It was an old black and white passport photograph; he recognised the face as that of the missing regular and noticed written on the back in biro was the name Jane with a date, 1972. He described to me the genuine fear he felt which caused him to race up the stairs and had to stand outside for some considerable time before he plucked up the nerve to re-enter the building to put the alarm on. He showed me exactly where the photograph had come from which was a crack in the ceiling and to this day has no idea how it got there or who put it there. Though this was obviously a disturbing experience he was at a loss as to what had happened to her and why the series of events had involved him. We decided to leave the cellar and after a fortifying drink arranged to meet again in a few weeks to take some photographs of the area. Knowing about the phenomena of apports (objects relating to someone who has passed which suddenly appear) I was convinced that someone in spirit had been trying to pass on a message to Craig. Despite this, being in that claustrophobic space made me uncomfortable and the story stuck with me for days after. I decided to follow it up and in doing so made an appointment at the births, deaths and marriages office run by the city council. I had a rough idea of the date of her apparent disappearance, May 2005, and a full name to go on and within minutes the relevant information was there in front of me. Jane had died at the beginning of May in hospital and nobody had known at that time. I felt saddened by the turn of events and freely admit I wondered if it was morally right to have pried into this. However I felt that she had tried to make contact with someone she probably thought of as a friend and had enjoyed socialising with and it eventually felt like the right thing to have done.

Some days later I made my way back to the Moorings as arranged to pass on this information and it came as no surprise to Craig as to the outcome of the search. We sat chatting in the bar and caught up with the latest happenings. However things had been quieter except for a strange recording taken in the bar after hours when voices were again heard angrily saying" get out". I got permission to spend some time in the cellar taking photographs but nothing unusual came out except a few orbs or light anomalies (more on this later) which appeared to be dust or other natural particles. We went over the incidents and I checked my notes to make sure they were accurate before we theorised on events. Craig felt that those who had passed over be it a previous landlord or regular still thought of the bar as being their place and maybe were not happy about some of the changes that had taken place. He felt in the case of Ted it was a benign playful presence but at other times had felt hostility which had perhaps been exacerbated by his curiosity and determination to find out what was causing the disturbances.

I tend to agree as I believe people do take ownership of the buildings they spent time in. We have all read about activity in castles for example where a historic family home has suddenly become a tourist trap or where someone has shown their displeasure over renovations. It must also be remembered that historically many unpleasant deeds were carried out in the vicinity and this negative energy will always be retained there giving the area at times a sense of inherent foreboding. I recently returned to the 'Moorings' for a catch up and was told that things appear to have 'quietened down'.

His Majesty's Theatre

One of the city's most vibrant and architecturally opulent buildings recently celebrated its centenary. Like any self respecting theatre its had its fair share of supernatural occurrences over the years with a number of spirit sightings who appear to have been 'one offs' to its most celebrated, that of 'Jake the ghost' or John Murray as he was known in this life. The building designed by Frank Matcham has undergone three periods of change in its life, in the 1930s, then in the 1980s when much of the stage area was modernised. The most recent addition is that of a restaurant and education facility housed in a contemporary glass structure, love it or loath it, it has divided opinion like nothing else in recent years. Since the theatre's opening night performance 'Red Riding Hood' in 1906 it has been a bastion of culture for the people of the city, playing host to innumerable stars from the golden age of theatre and cinema. Even during the hard times of the Second World War, when performances could stop mid flow due to bombing raids it has entertained and enthralled, and it is during this period that our story begins. During the Christmas period it was and still is customary to play host to a pantomime or similar family show, as was the case in December 1942 when the circus was in town. A circus in those days was an event guaranteed to generate excitement and during the war years it was not unusual for one to be held within the confines of a theatre rather than the 'big top' due to the black out. 'The Royal Britannic Circus' was well publicised in the local paper for weeks in advance proclaiming it as a 'colossal Christmas and New Year attraction'. Highlights included 'forest bred lions and three American spitfires', an equestrian act, a Russian troupe described as 'our allies' also 'performing pigeons', an eclectic mix if ever there was one. I find it difficult to imagine how they could have carried out the acts they did on stage but nevertheless they did much to the appreciative crowds, and it was by all accounts a roaring success. Unfortunately events took a tragic twist when on Christmas day an accident occurred at the theatre. The 'Press and Journal' of Monday the 27th

December contained the story stating 'tragedy in H.M. Theatre', a worker had been killed during a circus performance. The man in question was sixty nine year old John Murray who as a casual worker at the theatre had worked there for nearly twenty years as head fly-man. In those days there was not the emphasis on health and safety, with staff being hired on an ad hoc basis and equipment being dangerous by today's standards. On the night in question the horses which were an integral part of the show were being lowered in the aged lift from the stage, long since replaced, to the basement. No one is sure who made the decision to take all the horses down together, perhaps the men had wanted to finish up earlier, it was Christmas and families would be waiting, but whatever the reason, the decision was made to take all six horses down instead of the usual three. The men in the basement started turning the winch to lower the cage. The combined weight of the cargo proved too much and the lift plummeted sending the wheel spinning uncontrollably. John leaned forward to apply the break and was struck by the handle, revolving at such speed, that according to an eyewitness at the time, it, decapitated him. The death certificate tells a slightly different story citing the cause of death as a 'compound fracture of the skull and destruction of the brain.' Either way it must have been a terrible scene. Dougie Monaghan who started work at the theatre in 1938 as a page boy was there and witnessed the events as was colleague Dougie White who, in an effort to stop the wheel, was struck on the arm and badly injured. His compensation at the time for his injury was "two free tickets for life". Having heard previous accounts of these events I was prompted to visit the local library and after searching through December issues of the 'Press and Journal' 1943, stated as the date of the tragedy in some articles, I found nothing. Around a month later I had visited an auction and was lucky enough to be successful in my bid for a number of books, many of local interest. As there were so many it took some weeks before I had a chance to look in all the boxes. It was during a search that I came across some old newspaper clippings and noticed one was an article entitled 'eighty years of Christmas entertainment' and to my surprise in the entry for Christmas 1942 was 'The Royal Britannic Circus'. I returned to the library the next day and quickly discovered the article I had been looking for. Coincidence? Quite possibly, but I had the feeling I was guided to the correct date. I still feel that someone wanted me to give an account of the circumstances surrounding the tragedy and also of the man himself, who would probably rather be thought of as a once living and breathing person whose contribution was more than becoming a figure of lore. Facts are few given the time that has passed, but from the papers of the time and from the comments given by former colleagues we can gain a little insight into his life. John, as stated, had been with the theatre for many years and took a keen interest in all stage productions which visited Aberdeen. From a record he kept and carried about with him Mr Murray was able to recall details of every show which had appeared at His Majesty's since he joined its staff. It also stated that he left a widow, two sons and two daughters behind; his third son was tragically killed in action earlier in the year. In a strange quirk of fate, theatre archivist Edi Swan told me that he was giving a talk to the Women's Guild in the early 1980s and mentioned the ghost. He was surprised at the end of the talk to be approached by one of the women who said: "that's my father you were telling us about." Edi Swan is a gold mine of information on the theatre and the haunting having had a number of strange experiences himself, when as a young man in the late 1950s, he was employed along with other art school graduates as a scenic painter before becoming artistic director, a post he held for many years. His experiences have been written about previously in a number of books such as 'Theatre Ghosts' by Roy Harley Lewis and Norman Adams 'Haunted Neuk' but I feel they are worth mentioning again as they give evidence of the benign and helpful nature of 'Jake' as he has affectionately become known. When I met Edi recently he had his own theory on why places, especially theatres have such energies. He described to me how he likens it to a 'battery storing up all the emotions from performers and audiences alike', a gamut of emotions exist in the ether of these places and are at times tangible. This could be construed as residual energy and certainly when touring the infamous 'Lambeth Walk' I felt a cold spot which Edie pointed out was in direct line to the scene of the tragedy through the red painted brick wall in the corridor. It is unclear if any former staff members ever experienced anything unusual prior to Edi's experiences but what is known is that there have been distinct periods of activity. These have run from the late 1950s through to the 1980s when most of the original equipment was replaced by a more efficient and safe system, since the 1980s things quietened down only to start up again in more recent times, though in a more subtle manner. During the most recent upgrade workman claimed to have heard noises, but more on that later. During the initial period of activity the theatre still used much of its original equipment which no doubt played a part in creating the vast number of creaks and groans that would alarm staff working behind the scenes alone. Edi explained to me that he was aware of things being moved around while he was working late and would become frustrated by this however he was grateful for 'Jake's' intervention on two occasions. The first event occurred after Edi who, having sustained an ankle injury after a fall was forced to crawl to the basement in the hope of reaching the then accident and emergency unit at nearby Woolmanhill Hospital. The only means of exit in the area was kept locked at all times. However on this one and only occasion it was not, the padlock having been mysteriously opened. Bert Ewen, then manager, made it his duty to make sure everything was properly secured at night and swore at the time the door had been locked. The second incident occurred when Edi, after having a can of paint explode in his face and being temporarily blinded, was desperately trying to find the Prop Room sink to wash his eyes out. Being on the stage on his own there was a real danger of a fall into the orchestra pit but felt 'guided' and reached the sink safely, washing the paint away to no lasting damage. As we walked around the building we went down the 'Lambeth Walk' which is a passageway and series of steps running down to an exit at the side of the building. This area appears by all accounts to be the one where much of the activity has been centred with temperatures being noted at times to drop dramatically. It is cooler than other parts of the theatre and you could argue that being on the outer part of the building it would be, however it does not explain why in the early 1980s a security guard patrolling the area was stopped in his tracks as his Alsation dog's hackles rose, refusing to go into the area. I was aware of the temperature being particularly cold at the top of the passageway and sensed that someone was around, listening in to the conversation. It is difficult to explain but I felt an almost pleasant atmosphere despite the cold and have no doubt that the spirit in question is very kindly. I took a number of digital images for my records and caught a number of light anomalies on the stair, though I could not honestly say if it was the beginning of a spirit manifestation as some claim or from a more mundane source. Edi then took me backstage to the area where John's accident occurred and explained the purpose of the new equipment. I took more images near the scene of the accident which turned out to contain a vast amount of orbs though I am absolutely convinced that it was due to the dust in the air. We then looked at the area where John and his co-workers would play cards between duties. Though their bothy has long since gone it was interesting to get this background information. After some time in the basement we retraced our steps to the fly floor bridge, a walkway above the stage where much of the old equipment would have been situated. Edie explained that this area is also favoured by 'Jake' who was spotted there by the late Peter Thorpe a former stage manager. Peter had been surprised to meet an apparition wearing a "brown dust cost apron" who proceeded to walk towards him before disappearing. I became aware of movement across the walkway above the stage, a shadow that moved quickly out of sight and when I walked across to get a better view it had gone. I still don't know if I imagined it or perhaps it was a trick of the light but I could appreciate how easy it would be to let your imagination take over in this environment. The visit ended and we changed the subject, over coffee discussing the fate of another great Aberdeen theatre the Tivoli, again designed by Frank Matcham and sadly lying empty despite its former glories. Some time later I had the good fortune to put in touch with Kenny Luke who worked at the theatre for many years. In 1983 and still quite new to the building he was working an evening show when suddenly feeling a call of nature headed to the toilet at the back of the stairs despite being warned off the area by a number of old hands. Kenny takes up the story: "I went into the corridor, from a very hot backstage and walked into what I can only describe as a sensation of freezing cold water! I felt really uncomfortable, and at the same time heard the ground floor door which connects to the basement open. I waited to see who was coming up the stair, and when the time it takes to get to the level I was standing came, and no one appeared round the corner I hot footed it back to the stage pronto. When I got there, it was round interval and I was spied by Dougie Monaghan who, with a knowing smile, announced, take it you've just experienced Jake." He went on to say that his second experience of Jake came in 1992 when he was working during a run of 'Scotland The What'. "The stage manager Graeme Shepherd, who was running the corner (this is an area downstage left where all technical aspects of the show is controlled), turned to speak to me, looked upstage right, smiled, and beckoned me over, saying we have a visitor. I looked to where he was looking, and distinctly saw a dark shape move from the door, the same one as mentioned previously, to the upstage area. Concerned that it might be someone who shouldn't be there I went upstage to see if someone was heading towards the break room, again no one. Graeme and me both agreed what we saw, and put it down to unexplained." Kenny very rarely works there now but was told recently by Graeme Shepherd that there have been a number of incidents recently in the basement and cellar areas. Unexplained noises have been heard, figures caught out of the corner of the eye and equipment mysteriously moved. The feeling is that recent renovations have caused things to 'flare up'.

In June 2006 a number of articles appeared in the news concerning strange noises being heard in the theatre. David Steel, project manager was with three carpet fitters when they heard footsteps backstage. As they were the only people in the building there appeared to be no explanation. He went onto say that he had heard unexplained noises throughout the project and that" the guys were wary". Without meaning to sound pedantic I was somewhat annoyed by some of the reports which stated that a 'headless ghost' had returned to haunt the theatre. As far as I am aware know one has ever seen a headless ghost at the theatre, only ever seen fully intact in his infrequent appearances. I firmly believe that despite people's circumstances when passing over they are 'whole' on the other side and free of any disability that may have encumbered them in the physical life or indeed from the injuries that resulted in their death. I would suggest that in cases, for example, such as the ghost of Anne Boleyn which has been witnessed many times, headless, has been a recording or residual energy rather than a visitation from the next world to this.

There have been a number of events recently one of which was told to me by a friend whose sister used to work at the theatre. As one of the front of house staff she had arrived at work and was standing alone in the main auditorium when she became aware of a cold sensation she then felt herself nudged as if pushed slightly, turning quickly she noticed the drapes behind her started to move 'as if someone had walked by and brushed it'. She panicked and left the area rejoining colleagues who were at the front of the building. It came to light that others had experienced the feeling of a 'barrier' put in their way preventing them from moving forward though it must be said that they did not find the experience negative.

In the spring of 2007 two events occurred as a reminder of John's occasional visits. When 'Cats' began its run at the theatre staff were annoyed to find a number of costumes scattered on the floor when returning to work the next morning. Was this the work of Jake or a prank played by a work colleague? This incident was quickly followed by one slightly more unnerving when during 'lock up' two staff members were alarmed to hear seats on the floor above springing up even though there was no one there and knowing that it had been closed off during that evening's performance. I am in no doubt that John's spirit is still around though given the infrequency of his activities I would suggest that he has moved on and prefers to visit, perhaps to keep an eye on proceedings, make sure things are running smoothly and as the theatre starts its next hundred years is in safe hands.

Former Royal Bank of Scotland, Castle Street

This is one of the cities finest buildings and was built for use as a bank in1801 by architect James Burn designer of the infamous Bridewell prison. Originally housing The Aberdeen Banking Company and also at some point the Union Bank this elegant building sits on the corner of Castle Street and Marischal Street and now houses the Sheriff Court Annexe. Up until three years ago it remained as its' purpose intended though thankfully still retains the impressive interior by William Smith, the former banking area however has now been incorporated into the main public space of the court annexe. Interesting though this is, there was an earlier building on the site, which by contemporary accounts was even grander. There is little information available about this building, but what is known is that it was a house known as 'Pitfodels Lodging'. This building was the town house of the Menzies family of Pitfodels who for two hundred years, until 1635, were major players in the control of burgh affairs.

This building was erected about 1530 and by its description stood three floors high and turreted. On a grim note it has been thought that courtyard of Pitfodels Lodging was used to house one of Aberdeen's first means of public execution the 'Maiden'. The Scottish Maiden, essentially a forerunner of the guillotine was allegedly wheeled from there on execution days to the nearby 'heading hill' where justice was meted out swiftly no doubt to the delight of the blood thirsty crowds. The town, as with other executioners, employed someone with this task whose duties included 'soaping the rope' to allow the blade to fall swiftly and presumably to clean the machine afterwards. It has been recorded that this machine was used on a number of occasions on murderers and those who committed lesser crimes and although cited as being more humane than hanging it still induces an involuntary shudder when thought about. Records of the area before the banks' completion are scarce, though before the construction of Marischal Street in 1782 the Aberdeen residence of the Earls Marischal also stood nearby. It was from the window of this house that Mary Queen of Scots allegedly watched the execution of Sir John Gordon. Son of the earl of Huntly, beheaded after the battle of Corrichie in 1562. With all this history in the area, much of it violent, it is surprising that there has not been more 'stories' connected to the Castlegate area.

For me, one of the most interesting aspects of the former bank was what has been described as a 'cobbled area' in the cellar. Hidden below ground level, was, by all accounts the remains of an old road, apparently complete with pavements. But what were these remnants of an earlier age? Unfortunately this remains a mystery as the area in question was recently converted into holding cells during its recent change of use. Notwithstanding there have been rumours circulating about the Castlegate having secret tunnels/vaults beneath it for years and it is a fact that a number of premises in the area have bricked up entrances in their basements. The existence of an old bakery is one example 'which existed ten feet below the surface of Castle Street' and allegedly run by one Jacob Blackwell, though again how much of this is true, I cannot say. It is very intriguing nonetheless with shades of Edinburgh's South Vaults springing to mind.

The following story was related to me by a former colleague Duncan Haig. The following incident concerned a close friends' daughter, Adele, whose employment for the Royal Bank of Scotland on Castle Street provided a frisson not often associated with the banking profession. I have also included a personal experience garnered from visiting an adjoined building in Victoria Court which though momentary was fairly alarming at the time.

As a junior, Adele's duties included frequent trips to the storeroom to retrieve documents, a task she didn't like because of the 'atmosphere' in the basement. The filing cabinets in the basement were situated 'across the road'. The road, to explain, was the partial remains of an ancient cobbled street, still visible and running through one half of the basement. On one particular occasion, as she prepared to cross the road she found herself unable to do so, as if an invisible barrier had been placed in front of her. The caretaker who lived in the upper part of the building co-incidentally came down the stairs and finding Adele frozen to the spot enquired if she needed assistance. Adele described how she felt rooted to the spot and stating "I can't cross", remained stationary while the caretaker realising something was wrong retrieved the file. Adele could offer no rational explanation as to what had just occurred and was extremely upset by the incident. The caretaker as a means of response stated that his wife: "Did not like coming down here." When she returned home that evening her father, Bill, was aware of her upset and both he and his wife clearly recalled that: "She was very shaken," and was initially reluctant to talk to anyone about her experience in case "they laughed". She was told later that the road had originally led from the harbour to the gallows, historically situated in front of the Tolbooth. Whether this has any bearing on the incident is unknown, though it would appear that someone did not want her crossing the basement.

I was later contacted by Adele who kindly provided a fuller description of the basement area and was keen to point out that given the eerie surroundings was never enamoured to work there. She took solace in the fact that the caretakers cats would sometimes be there, having the run of the place they would provide occasional company though this provided small comfort. Adele mentioned part of the basement appeared to have been converted at some point: "However if you turned to the right the concrete floor ended and became dirty cobbles and there was a large, heavy wooden door in front of you. The door had a small window in it with bars like a prison cell and there were several more doors like this." Adele described the area as being like an alley that had been built over and was told that it had originally run all the way to the harbour and was possibly used as a route for prisoners who were to be transported. Whether this is historically accurate is open to debate however the area was obviously older than the building above and behind each door lay a 'cell'. Adele stated she had only ever been in the first two being described as: "Rough hewn rock, black with age, dirt or smoke," and intriguingly contained a number of locked wooden chests. The temperature changes between the two basement areas were also noticeably different and though there might be no overt supernatural explanation for this, it was noticeable enough to make the hair on Adele's neck rise which she was told was a normal physical reaction experienced by others. The caretakers' cats were also prone to act strangely in this area and would not step onto the cobbles preferring to pace the new concrete floor until the accompanied staff members had finished their duties. There behaviour was given credence by the fact that cats and dogs are particularly susceptible to spirit activity and can detect things that we are oblivious to, which seems a perfectly reasonable theory considering their odd behaviour. I was told: "It was also common to hear creaking doors, shuffling noises and a distinct feeling that someone else was there. I heard things and I felt things that I can't readily explain but they did me no harm."

Unfortunately the basement has changed completely having been converted into the aforementioned holding cells, with the cobbles now being hidden beneath concrete. Being told of this incident after the buildings' change of use, I never had the opportunity to visit therefore I was unable to garner any further information. Other than to muse that it was perfectly possible such a historic building would be home to an active spirit, I put it to the back of my mind. Little did I realise that fate would play a hand in allowing me access to another part of the structure in which I would personally experience something out of the ordinary and provide back up to Adele's story.

Around eight months after receiving Adele's description of events I was photographing the Shiprow area of Aberdeen and during my wanderings found myself overlooking an interesting old building. Hidden from view by a monstrous car park, which no doubt had replaced something more aesthetically pleasing in the not to distant past, I was excited to find this hidden gem. As it transpired the building in question was attached to what was the former bank and indeed had also been a bank on tow occasions. Peering through the now broken windows I stared in wonder at the elegant fireplace now on view and craned to get a better view through the shattered panes. The building albeit in a state of dilapidation was still the epitome of Georgian elegance, though now, home only to a huge and lively flock of pigeons. The said pigeons, on my approach fluttered en masse from the edifice alighting noisily nearby. Peering over the edge I became aware of the pond below, formerly known as Victoria Court, and went to investigate. With my interest peaked I decided to approach the council to establish who owned the property and in quirk of fate was told that there was a visit planned by the factor the next day.

I was given permission to have a look round but was told during the subsequent phone call to be aware that the building had been infested by pigeons and was therefore likely to be unpleasant, though in the end this turned out to be something of an understatement. I duly arrived the next day when the first indication that there was something unpleasant within became apparent. The factor on unlocking the premises was only able to partially open the front door due to a build up of pigeon excrement. This excrement sat directly behind the door and proved to be the ultimate draft excluder with the door creaking in protest before becoming entrenched in the crust. Squeezing in we found ourselves in what is best described as a lunar landscape of dried manure. Strange amorphous shapes peppered the hall and preceding rooms, with some sporting ancient nest like hats, set at a jaunty angle. As we crunched through decades of filth not daring to look too closely in the gloom or indeed at our feet the factor commented that this was probably the worst infestation he had ever seen a sentiment which I could not disagree with. The decades of accumulated filth was bad enough but worse still was the constant shrieking of the baby birds that crawled among the debris. The floors themselves were littered with hundreds of pigeons' corpses in various states of decay while all around others flapped furiously away on our approach, battering against glass in a frenzied attempt to escape. This was far the worst surroundings I had ever been in and my skin crawled at every turn. The rooms despite their condition still retained a modicum of elegance and were vast in scale, products of a by gone age.

After our tour of the ground floor rooms we approached the staircase, albeit in name only, as its resemblance to a ski slope did not go unnoticed. This was due to the same conglomeration of filth, reducing much of the steps to a gentle slope. 'Watch you don't slip' warned Nick, the factor, though we dared not seek purchase on splattered and crusted railing. I inwardly muttered a prayer of sorts and continued upwards. Though difficult to ascend we were eventually greeted by the attic and the uncommon sight of an adult hawk perched on an old fire extinguisher, casually feasting on the corpse of a freshly slain bird. Furious at being disturbed at its meal the hawk took to the air and in the claustrophobic atmosphere of the attic treated us to a heart stopping flyover before taking off through the nearest broken pane. Though repelled by the state of the building I was still impressed by the scale of the rooms, the beautiful plaster work and period features so often lost. It was like stepping into a time capsule and I did not waste the opportunity, clicking away furiously with my camera. I was astonished to learn that ten years ago the building had been in good repair but after vandals broke a number of widows allowing our feathered friends to enter, the rot had literally set in.

I was asked if I would like to see the basement, and we retraced our steps which proved even more hazardous on the way down. We headed towards the foreboding basement whose open doorway gaped like some hideous maw. A bloated mound of excrement stood sentry at the door while atop sat two furiously squawking, blind and naked baby birds. We crept by gingerly down the slope while the constant crunching of dirt or worse, under my feet caused all manner of horrible images to come flooding into my head. I repeated 'don't think about it like a mantra' which was of little comfort. It must be said that due to the surroundings I never once entertained the idea that the building would be haunted, having enough trouble instead, dealing with the physical. On reaching the basement I was astonished to find something akin to Adele's description of the adjoining bank including rough hewn cellars, cobbled walk way and a number of discarded cases, looking for all the world like small treasure chests though now containing the all encompassing filth. Pigeons shrieked as we crept ahead, the flash of my camera sending wild eyed, flurries rushing noisily into the air and most alarmingly round our heads. As I looked ahead Nick explained that there had been an extension added much later and was about to take me to what used to be the outside of the building when I became aware of a shadow detaching itself from the dark. Nick with his back to it remained unaware while I stared in fright over his shoulder, thankfully in the gloom he did not notice my startled expression. At that moment I must admit my heart Skipped a beat and I found myself gulping in a huge lung full of air. The shadow in possession of both arms and legs moved swiftly towards us and I inwardly cringed, screwing up my eyes as if in anticipation of a blow. The blow never came and when I opened my eyes a second later the figure had gone and we were alone. Given that Nick had the unenviable task of boarding up the various broken windows on his own I thought it prudent not to mention what had just transpired and remained silent. My breathing returned to normal and after continuing to outside of the building without further incident we returned up the stairs passing the still squawking sentries. I thanked him for his time and crunched my way out into the lane where I blinked in the bright sunlight and was grateful to say the least for being out of that hellish environment. I quickly checked my camera and among the many architectural images discovered I had captured two strange anomalies in the basement. The first appeared in one of the cells and took the form of a bright blue orb; the other even more intriguing was a bright light which appeared to be moving at speed. This image had been taken looking along the corridor in which the figure had appeared. It was noticeably different to the number of dust orbs in the vicinity and it was apparent that it was from an entirely different source but what it was, I cannot say with certainty.

Incidentally, on the other side of the lane is a canteen also built on the site of Pitfodels lodging, which is used by bus drivers. I had gone there to leave some questionnaires concerning the Captain Beaton story and in conversation with one of the workers, Susan, I mentioned the fact I had been taking photographs in the old bank. She laughed, stating: "Oh that place, its meant to be haunted." Unfortunately how she knew this remains a mystery as she did not elaborate further only to say it was common knowledge, indeed, she went on to mention that a figure had also been spotted within the canteen on occasion though not by her personally. I thanked her and left deciding to visit the library to try and find out more about who had lived or worked there. Disappointingly I could find very little information other than in the 1850s, a William Bain, the manager of the then Royal Bank of Glasgow resided their followed sometime later by a local printer George Cornwall who ran his business from there. After that the trail went cold as later directories only referred to it as 54 Castle Street until in recent memory it became the Clydesdale Bank. The surrounding area also had a number of interesting concerns at one point including, in close proximity, a brewery, ironically now home to a 'wet hostel'. I had reached a dead end if you forgive the pun, and having been unable to re visit the location, so far, have been unable to add any more substance to the story.

On a final note, perhaps the two most positive aspects of this visit, for me, is that I had the opportunity to capture the interior of one of the cities last intact buildings before the developers moved in. I also, now have, a fairly accurate picture of what the cellars of the Bank of Scotland may have looked like during Adeles tenure, and believe me they must have been pretty eerie though I daresay a lot cleaner. The cells, at one time, would no doubt have held many important documents from Aberdeen's leading citizens. The cobbles in the basement, still intact, were perhaps remnants of a more ancient building. But what of the figure, was he connected to the bank, the printers, the brewery or perhaps someone involved in swift justice? It is all conjecture but I know what moved towards me was a recognisable figure and in that heart stopping moment these questions were the last thing on my mind.

Dunecht Estate

A former colleague of mine, Paula, told me this interesting story which took place in Aberdeenshire. Though nothing physically was seen, something was definitely heard and until the stories coda, bore all the hallmarks of a residual haunting.

In her teenage years Paula was involved in a local pony club and spent much of her spare time participating in competitions and show events and depending on the location of the event and its duration, this would sometimes involve a sleep over. The equestrian event took place approximately twelve miles west of Aberdeen on the Dunecht estate and the participants arrived the previous day as was customary. The house itself was built for the Earl of Crawford in 1820 and remains the centrepiece of what is still the largest estate in Aberdeenshire. The house, an incredibly imposing building, dominates the surrounding area and you would be forgiven for thinking this is where the story took place, however this is not the case. Instead it took place in a rather innocuous looking out building, the old wash house, situated some distance from the house at the end of a long drive. This Victorian construction, used by staff, at a time when the estate employed a large number of workers, had lain empty for many years. The machinery once so frequently used was now gone and the building, partially derelict, lay empty apart from occasional usage by Aberdeenshire pony club. The club, long established, had used the facility for overnight accommodation for some time and participants involved in both club camps and training days were expected to 'rough it'.

On this particular occasion Paula and a group of eleven friends were participating in a weekend event and as seniors were allowed to stay in the upstairs part of the building. The sleeping quarters were directly above the locked 'tuck shop' which was only used on occasion and kept locked at all times. Though the surroundings were basic it was seen as an adventure and sleeping on camp beds added to the fun for the boisterous teenagers.

During our conversation, Paula explained that she had heard stories concerning the wash house for some time but suspected it was all 'leg pulling', designed to frighten the younger participants prior to an overnight stay. The most oft repeated of these tales appeared to be that of strange feelings experienced by those in the building and of unexplained noises coming from no discernible source. People had also mentioned how strange noises were often heard from the loft but like the others did not pay these much heed.

The group, after setting up for the event, had bedded down for the night and were lying awake chatting when one of the males in the group pointed out that he had heard someone downstairs. They listened in silence and became aware of the sound of footsteps slowly ascending the stairs. When a brave volunteer got up to investigate and looked out onto the darkened staircase, the noise abruptly stopped. Further investigation showed the building to be empty apart from those remaining on the top floor. As the downstairs door was locked they knew that there could be no one else in the building and somewhat disconcerted, returned to the main group who by now were huddled together, who with voices now audibly lowered, discussing what had just taken place. They settled down in their sleeping bags once more, attempting to relax, only for the noise to start up again. The sound of shuffling footsteps started up again and ascended the stair, stopped abruptly on the large corner step outside the door, twisted, then stopped suddenly. Paula recalled that it sounded like: "Work boots walking on earth or grit." The group, by now huddled in silence, listened as the steps continued their slow progress, stopping for a few seconds then once again starting. The group still frozen with fear could barely contain their alarm and clung to each other till suddenly the sound stopped. Having had to endure the continuous soft shuffling sounds which appeared to have gone on for an age, the relief was palpable. Fear was soon replaced by nervous laughter bordering on hysteria. Like survivors from some particularly grim ordeal the babbled excitedly before someone urged them to 'hush, in case it came back'.

No one could sleep and they remained awake, to scared to communicate in anything above a whisper in case something else was 'stirred up'. Huddled together and chatting in hushed tones, they remained together until the welcome morning light shook them into action. They debated as to who or what had caused the noises and eventually agreed it must have been a ghost. Paula's friend, Chris, in an effort to make light of the situation named the 'ghost' Bob which lifted the mood slightly. The events, during the night, though not forgotten, was certainly put to the back of the competitors minds as the club prepared for competition and in the cold light of day more pressing thoughts came to bear.

To bring this particular story to its conclusion, Paula told me, that later in the year, "Us seniors were helping out with the juniors (in the wash house) and we opened the tuck shop door downstairs, scratched on the inside of the door was the word Bob, the door was old and heavy and always locked and no one had access to it." Paula has never forgotten this and when asked what she feels about it today, stated: "I still get goosebumps".

No one knows who is present in the wash house, it is rarely used unless for club events, though Paula was told later that there were rumours of a worker being killed there in an accident many years ago.

Crathie

The following incident was related to me by my partner Carol and her friend Sandra Stewart and took place in the summer of 2005. During the year they had often talked of having a weekend away to recharge their batteries and subsequently discovered that there was a company that specialised in Tipi weekends. The idea appealed to all and a weekend away was booked. The retreat was located at Crathie near Ballater and the group instantly fell in love with their surroundings, such was the tranquil atmosphere of the area. They were shown to a field adjacent to the owner's cottage where they set up camp. Having around eight individuals present, and being such a large party, they were accommodated in the two largest tents, which stood like pyramids in the hazy sunshine. The area itself, apart from being incredibly beautiful, had a number of geographic points of interest in the vicinity and the owner was happy to share this information on the grand tour, pointing out the nearby Gallows Hill and Craig nam Ban: the women's or witches hill which lay brooding in the distance.

The group spent the first day exploring, walking and climbing, scaling the nearby peak known locally as the witches hill. This hill, according to records, was the site of the last witch to be burned in Scotland and the group shivered involuntarily as they passed the site. As the day wore on they returned to camp, ready to deal with more mundane matters, preparing the evening meal and lighting the fire. After dinner and the requisite washing up the group were relaxing round the fire when both Sandra and Carol decided to go outside to look around. It was such a beautiful clear night that the sky was alive with stars and the pair stood and gazed in awe. It was around ten in the evening and as they shone torches into the night sky, a movement in the field caught their eye. Sandra, sensing this movement brought her torch to bear and shone it directly into the field, illuminating a moving figure.

Sandra related the following: "I saw a figure dressed in a monk's garment with a hood pulled far over his head, I saw no face, his hands were crossed and hidden in the sleeves of the garment." She drew Carol's attention to the figure and they both froze, momentarily shocked, watching in silence. The figure was "gliding and hovering above the ground with a green shimmery area where he was gliding." The monk remained visible for ten to fifteen seconds, following him, albeit gingerly through the field before it vanished. I was told, they were shining a torch on the figure the whole time and could see him very clearly despite the area out with the beam being very dark.

They followed him for some distance, but feeling 'shakey' and with 'the hairs on their neck standing on end' decided to return to the tent where they recounted their experience to the wide eyed audience. Though not particularly frightened, Sandra did feel a 'a bit shocked' by the turn of events and the tale roused the group from their after dinner torpor into action. Babbling excitedly, some ran outside hoping to see the figure while the less brave remained huddled within their sleeping bags. The figure of course had gone and after some minutes they settled down, though somewhat uneasily, for the night.

In the morning they inspected the field which being expansive and completely flat afforded no hiding place or dip in which someone could have hidden. In the cold light of day, they wondered if they should broach the subject with the owners and after some debate decided to approach them. There was still the nagging suspicion that it was some kind of elaborate practical joke, played for the benefit of unsuspecting customers and therefore it seemed the only course of action open to them. This theory was quickly quashed, and they were told in no uncertain terms that the owners had been unaware of what had transpired, however, it was pointed out that others had seen a similar figure in the same area. It came as no surprise to Carol when the owner pointed out that directly down the hill lay the ruined foundations of a very ancient chapel known as St. Columba and it is assumed that the monk had been connected to this chapel.

By all accounts the area has a magical atmosphere and it would appear that spirit visitors are occasionally sensed 'passing through' and going about their business. The current owner is keen to point out that the area has a peaceful atmosphere and though occasional 'visitations' occur, they are non-frightening. The occasional footsteps or sensing of a presence seem to be part of the fabric of the area and given its ancient history, this comes as no surprise.

Ma Cameron's Inn

Cameron's Inn is one of Aberdeen's oldest and most beloved pubs. It was built on the site of a much older establishment, known as Sow Croft Inn, and it is assumed that they kept pigs there. The keeping of livestock was a common practice at the time with many families owning at least a few animals. The Sow Croft Inn existed at a time before Union Street was built and it has been suggested it sat atop a natural incline, which would have run all the way to the Green. St. Nicholas Kirk, situated in close proximity, would have been a magnet for foraging animals, as pigs, which naturally root for food, had the habit of disinterring corpses. It is known that this caused enough of a problem for a bylaw to be passed banning people from letting their animals forage in the grounds of the kirk under pain of a heavy penalty. One can imagine that the owner of the Sow Croft Inn must have had his work cut out, keeping a wary eye on his wandering swine.

Sow Croft was eventually replaced by a coaching inn, where it was noted, that horses from as far away as Huntly were stabled, under the management of then owner John Ross. In the late 1800s the family most associated with the inn took over, the Camerons, and it was John Camerons wife Amelia who earned the homely soubriquet of 'Ma'. The family continued to run the pub till 1933 when it was eventually taken over by Alex Mitchell. During the Cameron family's tenure, it should be noted, 'Ma's' was an elite howff, and catered for a well heeled class of citizen. This was due to their policy at that point, of not selling draught beer, considered a lower class drink.

The pub as we know it today has undergone many changes. Initially a lot smaller, with stables at the rear, it traded solely at number six Little Belmont Street before incorporating its neighbour, number eight. This building, originally a whole sale store, had remained so for many years until relatively recently, when the enterprising owners incorporated it into the pub.

For many years I had heard stories concerning a spirit presence in the pub. These included an account by a decorator who had been spooked by strange knocking sounds, while working alone. I had always been intrigued by this story and wishing to know more, I approached the current manager Jason for his comments. I had the opportunity to meet with him soon after and we met in the snug, the oldest and most atmospheric part of the pub. In conversation, it came to light, that there had been a number of incidents which had occurred during his employ, including those involving colleagues, who had complained of being watched or followed. Jason explained that he was aware of the stories circulating among staff but was not directly involved. This however changed when on one particular evening the following incident of note occurred. It transpired that after he had finished his shift, and after joining the other staff on duty for a drink in the snug, he recalled the following: "We were sitting having a quiet chat when suddenly a few of us noticed a dark figure out of the corner of our eyes moving past the serving hatch towards the door that leads to the toilet. Thinking a customer had been locked in I went to search for them and discovered no one in the corridor, I then checked the toilets in case some one was hiding in them, again no one. I went through the entire bar and returned to the snug, we deliberated whether it was our imagination or not."

Jason returned to work and I had the opportunity to speak to other employees who had either experienced something out of the ordinary themselves or had heard rumours from others. There was however the usual disagreement, as some claimed over active imaginations were the probable cause while others, who had first hand experiences, disagreed. It was also noted that the activity appeared to follow no particular pattern of behaviour, the incidents being sporadic and its manifestation occurring in different parts of the building.

After further conversations, it came to light, that that the activity appeared to be particularly prevalent in three locations. Firstly, the original area of the stables, secondly, the front lounge of what was originally the whole sale store at number eight and lastly on the top floor of number six which was once used as accommodation for staff. It was noted that feelings noted in these areas were best described as uneasy, as testified by one of the bar staff who stated: "Its not funny when you are on your own and the lights keep getting switched on and off." She went on to describe, that recently when changing a barrel in the tap room, she was suddenly aware of someone standing directly behind her and was too scared to turn round, "I just stood still till whatever it was left and when it felt safe to turn round I got out quick." Despite a colleague putting this down to an overactive imagination, she has remained adamant that there was someone there, observing her.

After a few weeks had lapsed I returned to Cameron's, to try and meet those I had missed first time round, and again met up with Jason. He immediately mentioned, that a regular, Alistair, had been sitting having a pint in the snug, and being the only one in the bar was sitting near the serving hatch, staring ahead. Noticing movement from the corner of his eye, he glanced through the serving hatch and saw a beer tap turn itself on and proceed to pour a drink. The staff member, on duty at the time, had briefly left the bar and was unaware of the incident until Alistair called out and returning quickly, he promptly switched the tap off. However, both were shocked and left practically speechless as the tap turned itself on, twice more, in quick succession. To emphasise the point I was shown that it takes a certain amount of strength to turn the tap on and was therefore unlikely to have been caused by a fault in the mechanism. I was told that on all other occasions it worked perfectly well. I left the bar not wishing to impose further, encouraged by the latest information I had received.

A number of days later I had the good fortune to mention my visit to a work colleague Mike. As it transpired, Mike had been a regular of the pub for years and did not seem surprised at the stories I regaled him with. It turned out, that in a strange quirk of fate, the witness to the beer pouring incident in question, was a good friend of his. I was assured that his friend was not prone to flights of fancy and was certain of what he had witnessed. Things were certainly looking up when Mike mentioned that he was on friendly terms with previous owners, the Bruce family, who up until recently had owned the pub, since the 1970s. I did not take much persuading when he mentioned it would probably be of value if I could speak to them and as luck or fate would have it Mike was given the contact number of Alison Bruce which he duly passed on to me. After an initial feeling of trepidation I contacted Alison and was relieved to find that far from being adverse to discussing this, was extremely interested in what I was trying to achieve, providing me with some valuable and fascinating information.

She related the following: "The most reliable incident was an account by Mr. Masson who was locked in and painting the ceiling of number eight. He had heard three knocks from above and returned three knocks with his paintbrush. Three knocks from above were then returned. He was so spooked he left the building. The flat above number eight was empty and had not been used for years, the only access was through a window in the lane, the incident occurred in the early hours of the morning." She went on to say the other incident of note happened to Elaine who was employed part time and was sent to get crisps. The crisp boxes were on the top floor of number No.6. She thought someone had followed her into the room and was chatting to them. When they didn't reply she turned round to see why. There was no one there. She ran down the stairs and was very white and shaken." Alison went on to say that when she saw Elaine's face: "I had shivers up my spine, I also had shivers when Mr. Masson told me what happened. I have felt a presence on many occasions while I was working in the pub. It's not been an evil presence, but never the less I have been spooked on dark nights or dark mornings." She concluded, by saying: "The cleaner Charlene thought she saw a figure when she was cleaning what used to be the stable area early one morning."

I was very grateful for her input as the family had owned the pub for many years and had consistently been aware of a presence throughout their ownership. It was interesting to note that current staff were experiencing the same phenomena as experienced by former employees. I felt, that again, it further strengthened the argument that the pub is still being visited by spirit on occasion. But the question remains, who is the spirit that visits Cameron's? I sense that whoever it is, is not permanently grounded as having visited the building on numerous occasions I have been unaware of any presence suggesting that activity may only occur sporadically. It is also unlikely to be a residual recording, as the activity appears to diverse to be a recording, and does not follow a set pattern as is often the case in residual phenomena. Equally unlikely is a grounded spirit, as I believe if they were permanently at home there, then the activity would occur more frequently. For me the most likely answer would be a person or indeed persons who had a close link to the Inn, perhaps a previous owner, someone who likes to check up on thing periodically and is not adverse to playing a few practical jokes. Though there appears to be no malice intended, incidents like these do cause alarm. It is the fear of the unknown which frightens us, the intangible that cannot be rationally explained which we are all prey to and in that respect I can understand why staff have felt uneasy.

On a final note, I remembered an incident, which I had forgotten about until recently, of an occasion when I had visited Cameron's. One Friday evening, as my partner and I sat in the snug I became acutely aware of someone wanting to make his presence felt, who impressed the name John onto my mind as well as a visual description of himself. He appeared in my mind to be dressed in clothes from the late 18th century, waistcoat, breeches and tailcoat. He definitely had a strong connection to the building and his presence remained with me for a number of minutes. It was only much later, when I realised that one of the original owners was called John Ross that I entertained the possibility that perhaps he might be responsible for the activity. I would really love to know.

Commerce Street

The following story was related to me by a work colleague and took place when she first moved to Aberdeen. The paranormal activity was mainly aural rather than visual but none the less terrifying for her and other family members. Diane had been on the look out for a flat to buy and was soon lucky enough to find one that suited her needs in Commerce Street. This street, situated near the harbour is pretty much like any other, consisting of a long row of undistinguished tenements with shops below, once home to the Northern Co-operative. Built around a hundred years ago they now sit alongside more contemporary business premises. At first glance the area seems pretty nondescript, however one has only to look at the city's past to realise that this was not always the case. The immediate area has a very dark history, possibly more so than anywhere else, and this may go some way to explaining the phenomena that Diane witnessed.

Looking at city plans of Aberdeen from the eighteenth and early nineteenth century, it shows the street to now occupy what was a natural valley running towards the harbour, with Castlehill on one side and Heading Hill on the other, the area is synonymous with the barbaric practice of public executions. Commerce Street itself also has the unenviable reputation as being the site of witch burnings, though there is debate as to exactly where on the hill these took place. What is known though, is that, for example, in the year 1597, twenty three women and one man were burned at the stake.

In more enlightened times a number of schools and churches sprang up as well as businesses such as the aforementioned Northern Co-operative, which included a draper and ironmonger, and so it remained for many years until the redevelopment of the area. With the subsequent widening of the dual carriageway on Virginia Street much of the older buildings were swept away to accommodate the increased traffic leaving the row of tenements, remnants of a time gone by.

It was in this setting that Diane and her cousin moved into the first floor flat. At first all was quiet, until late Autumn when a series of curious events unfolded. In conversation, Diane recalled it was on a Wednesday evening around seven when the first signs of paranormal activity took place.

Diane takes up the story: "I was sitting in the living room at the front of the building watching television. A normal mid week evening, I was feeling relaxed when the room temperature dropped and what I can only describe as a line of voices sounded, they were both talking and chanting but not in English." She went on to explain: "It sounded like it was in Latin and the voices seemed to move across the top of the room, going round the ceiling before stopping." Diane, panicking, left the room quickly and described her reaction: "My hair stood on end, my heart was racing, instinctively I knew these sounds were not from a normal source. I ran to the kitchen and paced the floor knowing that I would have to return to the room, I tried to rationalise it, made tea and plucking up the courage to return, did so, where everything including the temperature was back to normal." She explained that though the flat 'never had a cosy feel to it' this was the something much more potent. In due course, life in the flat returned to normal and the incident was all but forgotten, until one evening when Diane had a few friends over, and again the same chain of events started up. The temperature dropped and the voices speaking in what appeared to be Latin were heard in the room, again from no discernible source. Her visitors became so alarmed that she found herself explaining to a male friend that it was probably a taxi radio causing interference through her stereo, even though she was certain it was not plugged in. She continued the ruse till they left, then reluctantly checked the stereo, verifying it was, indeed unplugged.

In an effort to find out the history of the building she began casually asking people about the area and was told from various sources that there had been murders committed there years ago and even further back there had been a witches coven. It is true that there had been a murder in the 1960s in the vicinity, though not in the actual building, and indeed there had been rumours of witchcraft in the past. This however is conjecture, as the executions themselves are the only facts we know to be true, and in any case Diane considered these theories inadequate. In more enlightened times it is generally acknowledged that "witches" of old were probably no more than poor unfortunates, accused of the black arts after falling out with neighbours, guilty of nothing more than eccentricity at worst. They paid a heavy price for being 'different'. It goes without saying that the idea of covens practising in the area is probably a myth and has never been substantiated through records.

We theorised, that though colourful, these stories had probably nothing to do with the actual events, and I hazarded a guess that given the dark history of the area, the chanting would most likely be due to residual sounds from the past. Everything again returned to normal and Diane who describes herself as 'pretty level headed' tried to rationalise the events though she could find no explanation. Another puzzling phenomenon was that 'old fashioned Kirby grips' kept appearing on the carpet, being found throughout the flat. Diane had first noticed them when she had moved in and despite thoroughly cleaning the flat they continued to appear from nowhere at odd intervals. This fact was verified by relatives, who when staying there, remarked on how often the grips kept appearing, causing Diane no end of consternation. The flat continued to have an 'unsettled feeling' to it, and despite living there for some time she could not settle. Eventually, this uneasy feeling was partially instrumental in her selling up and moving on.

An interesting coda to the story occurred soon after, when during my research, Diane had volunteered to show myself and two others, the location of said flat. As she recounted the story, and unbeknown to her, one of the group, Rob, mentioned that a close friend of his, James, had lived for some time in a flat in the next tenement block. We listened intently as he explained that his friend's rented flat was considered to be haunted and that the atmosphere was considered unpleasant. Friends began to make excuses for not visiting, including Rob himself who 'did not like the stairs', however more concrete phenomena soon followed.

The first event of note occurred when James had been busy ironing one evening. This usually mundane task was brought to a standstill when on leaving the room briefly to answer the phone, returned to find that the white shirt he had been ironing had disappeared. He searched the room and was described as being 'incredibly puzzled', stopping to try and retrace his movements. After wracking his brains, he concluded that perhaps he had done it already, after all he had ironed other shirts that were identical. He put it to the back of his mind and had forgotten the incident until one day when checking the fuse box he was astonished to find a white shirt, dust covered and crumpled, stuffed into the corner of the box. There was no explanation to be had and after that he began to feel on edge during the times he was in the flat, preferring to be out whenever possible.

The second most obvious event, and the one that finally convinced him of a supernatural presence, occurred soon after. As is the case with many accounts, the evening leading up to the event had been nondescript, and after watching television, Jim, decided to call it a night and went to bed. The night passed uneventfully, and after rising, he went through to the living room to have a cup of tea and a cigarette. The first thing he noticed was that during the night something had opened his cigarettes and scattered them about the living room floor, though on closer inspection he realised that they had not been scattered, but rather arranged, into a 'pattern'. He could find no explanation as he had left them, unopened, on the television the night before. He was convinced, there was no way they had found themselves on the floor through natural means and Rob explained that after finding out about this, friends stopped going round altogether because of the 'weird atmosphere'. Jim moved out soon after.

The events in Commerce Street remain unexplained, and as I would describe both Diane and Rob as reliable, I cannot see any other explanation than that of paranormal activity.

In retrospect one possible explanation for the phenomenon could be that of an apport, a term for the seemingly random appearance of objects. An apport is acknowledged as being a genuine spirit phenomenon and is thought to be a sign of someone wishing to communicate by manifesting an object that has significance to either the person in spirit or whoever is in receipt of the communication. It is interesting to note that this may explain the appearance of the Kirby grips though Diane did not understand how this could be relevant to her. The Latin chanting is far more intriguing, and after some thought I felt comfortable enough to put forward the theory, that this was a recording in the fabric of the area, most likely associated with the witch burnings. It has been noted that during executions a priest would be given the task of performing the last rites, a prayer for those about to meet their end, and was more than likely in Latin. This is only a theory but as far as I am concerned is the only viable one. Given the varied phenomena in the two flats an argument could also be made for both poltergeist activity as well as residual phenomena and given the dark history of the area this comes as no surprise. As both parties mentioned have since left Commerce Street it is unknown whether the activity still continues.

Morrone Lodge

An outdoor pursuit centre is probably one of the last places you would expect to be haunted but as you will see, appearances can be deceptive. The lodge existed for many years as a hostel for visiting community groups, and team building events and continued as such until recently when Aberdeenshire Council sold the building to a private company for conversion into housing. The lodge, a substantial granite building is situated on the outskirts of Braemar, and with panoramic views of the surrounding countryside it is the perfect location for walkers and those wishing to blow the cobwebs of city life out of their systems. As the building's usage recently changed, I did not get the opportunity to visit personally but was given the following account by Annie McIntosh. Annie, who along with other community worker colleagues, stayed at the lodge a number of years back participating in a team building exercise, and her experiences form the basis of the following. It is worth mentioning, at this point, that she knew very little of the building's reputation at the time, and only subsequently found out that others had experienced the same unsettling phenomena she bore witness to.

The group, numbering around eight, had arrived at the lodge after the drive from Aberdeen. Amid the banter and excitement of the weekend ahead, they began to decide on who should sleep where, and after dumping their rucksacks and belongings in the dormitories, they met up in the communal living room. Everything appeared normal at first, and they spent some time exploring the building. After being assigned tasks, the group split up, some going outside, while others remained indoors. Annie, who had remained inside, began to feel an uneasy sensation, nothing particularly tangible, but the feeling of wanting to get out of the building became very strong. Eventually she did, putting the feelings of unease down to the new environment, after all the area was deathly quiet and the lack of background noise took some getting used to. Outside, in the sunlight, everything felt normal and all was forgotten until later when she ventured back inside. Again, she began to feel a change in the atmosphere, an almost imperceptible feeling, but one never the less which made her anxious. Being alone in the lodge began to prey on her imagination and she began to regret not going out to the village with the others. She became aware of someone moving softly about the building and knowing she was alone, felt genuine fear. In conversation, she stated that: "The other folk were due back soon but I ran out and all the way down to the village."

Trying to put things in perspective, and after meeting up with the others who had been out exploring, she returned to the lodge. Not looking forward to bedtime due to the 'atmosphere' in her dormitory, she decided to stay up as long as possible, but eventually became too tired to participate further and decided to retire for the night. Some of the group continued to chat, planning their activities for the next day, until they too decided to call it a day and retired to the dorms. Despite her earlier fears and the all encompassing silence, she promptly fell asleep. Some time later she woke to find the room pitch black and the sound of movement from the bed above. She recalled: "I felt that there was someone moving in the bed above me and there was noises of the duvet folding, I sat tight but was terrified." In the morning all was quiet and she double - checked to see if anyone had decided to swap beds in the middle of the night, which they hadn't, as it lay undisturbed. Fortunately for Annie, the following night passed without further incident, though it transpired that during the course of their visit, the same noises were reported by others, at various times of the day and night.

Shortly, after returning to Aberdeen, Annie casually mentioned the incident to a colleague Christine, who had visited the lodge on a previous occasion. Christine recalled, to Annie's surprise, that during one of her stays, she had awoke to find a figure standing at the foot of the bed, described as 'a doctor figure, tall with a large moustache and wearing a dark jacket'. Disturbingly, as word got around, other visitors in the community network began to tell their stories in which the common description appeared to be that of seeing shadowy figures, in the dorms. This was accompanied, on occasion, by a feeling of being pushed down into the bed. Needless to say, the recipients found this, very frightening.

Other stories began to creep out of the woodwork, workers who had kept their experiences to themselves until now, began to feel comfortable about unburdening themselves. Perhaps it wasn't down to imagination after all, they concluded. Visitors, who had bought dogs with them claimed how upset they became, being agitated and unable to settle. This was particularly prevalent in the living room area, where their behaviour was described as, being aware of a presence that remained unseen to the human eye. Another frequently reported phenomena, was that of footsteps which were frequently heard on the stairs when there was no one in the area. This was witnessed by Doug, a former colleague of Annie's, who was certain that everyone was in bed on the ground floor, when he heard steps from above. On a more sinister note Annie had heard of a youth group of 'hard nuts' 17, 18 and 19 year olds who ended up terrified after holding a séance, feeling there was an 'evil presence' in the living room. On reflection Annie stated that during both incidents she was 'really uncomfortable and felt real fear', she is certain that there have been things that happened there and that there is still some kind of 'residue' and although describing the lodge as a great place, she felt: "The atmosphere was not right." Perhaps, she conceded, some of the 'activity' may have been due to imagination, but: "Other folk were really convinced that there was something in the building." and given the amount of witness reports, who am I to disagree?

I subsequently spent some time looking for clues as to the history of Morrone Lodge. Records are almost non existent as to the building's original purpose but it has been recorded that in the early 1900s it was used as an isolation hospital or as it was more accurately described in records a 'fever hospital'.

On a last note, there are many who claim that their pets, particularly cats and dogs, at times, appear to be aware of an unseen presence. This is a perfectly reasonable assumption, and is arguably, one of the most common indications of a spirit being present. After all, how many times have you seen your pet stare intently at an empty space in a room, or become agitated, and in the case of dogs, begin to bark excitedly when there is no one there?

Orbs

"Orbs" are perhaps the most misunderstood, and at times, most unexplainable phenomena to occur in years, and there are as many supporters as detractors as to their legitimacy. Opinions vary as to what is thought, by some, to be genuine evidence of the first stages of spirit manifestation. However there is certainly no evidence, at least scientific evidence, to back this claim up. Photography was still relatively new when the first 'spirit photographs' were taken. In keeping with the Victorian aesthetic of the time, well at least according to the available photographs, the favoured mode of appearance by spirit was to pose in the usual staid manner of the period. Family portraits, with shrouded spirit relatives in attendance, certainly exemplified what the Victorians construed as otherworldly. Unfortunately as time passed it came abundantly clear that many spirit photographers were charlatans playing on the emotions and fears of a pious society. It came to light during preceding court cases, that the ingenious use of models and props were used to create these romanticised and gloomy images. Employing tricks, like double exposure, to create suitably ethereal images, proved irresistible to what was thought of as an enlightened upper middle class.

As someone with firm beliefs, and an advocate of spiritualism, it is not my intention to cast aspersions on the character of every one of those early pioneers, but it must be said that many exponents of spirit photography faked their images. As you can imagine this did spiritualism no favours, as some had blatantly mislead the public. For profit or fame, the guilty were publicly shamed and in some cases jailed. Despite many notable scandals, the trade in spirit photography flourished, people still wanted to believe, and there are many examples, which sceptics could not disprove being noted. Though the obvious trickery employed by some was doing a great disservice to the movement, I would argue that not everyone involved in early spirit photography was faking their images, and there are historically many good examples where exponents have demonstrated their gifts and appear to be genuine. As is often the case it was unfortunate that many were tarred with the same brush.

As technology progressed and the use of cameras became the norm, the volume of images increased leading to some fine examples of apparitions captured on film. Interestingly many of the best examples were taken unknowingly and appear to be a case of being in the right place at the right time. Things really took off with the invention of the highly sensitive digital camera, some would argue, too sensitive, as it has the propensity to pick up all manner of airborne particles, and in many cases ruining a fairly decent family snap. It was at this time the 'orb' began to appear. Though seen occasionally, when using a standard 35mm camera, they were now everywhere, floating in our rooms, in the park, in front of your Auntie's head, everywhere. 'Orbs' are essentially balls of light thought by many to be the first sign of spirit manifestation; you only have to look on the internet to see there are thousands of sites dedicated to the phenomenon. But what exactly are they? To date there is insufficient evidence to back up the claims that they are spirit energy though many do appear in alleged haunted locations. They come in a variety of sizes and shapes from perfect circles to oblongs, crescents to indistinct blobs, you name it the list is endless. I remember when I took my first 'orb' photograph and how excited I felt, only to discover sometime later that if I rubbed my curtains together, disturbed the dust, took a shot, then hey presto! 'Orbs' I was most disappointed. This is not to say that they all come from such mundane sources. Yes, they can be captured when light bounces off insects, leaves, pollen, but on occasion they are less explicable. Many researchers have made the claim that they, are a sign of supernatural activity and although in some cases this may be true, in the majority, I feel not. It is worth noting that until digital cameras became common, 'orbs' were quite rare, and it perhaps due to the sensitivity of these cameras that we now see an abundance of these images. So how do we tell a real 'orb' from a false one, as I believe there are two distinct kinds. False 'orbs' tend to be very pale in colour and transparent which unfortunately accounts for around 95% of my images, but what of the others? They are certainly worth more serious consideration and can appear in vivid colour, deep red, green, purple or solid and bright and in the best instances appear to be moving or are ectoplasmic in appearance not unlike a mist. Mediums point out the significance of colour in their work and how it denotes feelings and moods and it could go some way to explain the vast array of hues that have been captured on film. Perhaps the camera is picking up the emotions associated with a certain spirit? In the event of an ectoplasmic form appearing on film, care must be taken when analysing the image, as for example, breathe on a cold day being captured or smoke, which again, can give this appearance and lead to a false image.

The most interesting examples of spirit photography, are the ones where anomalies appear at the same time as the 'feelings' associated with spirit begin to manifest. An example of this was during my two visits to Powis house, where I was aware of a strong presence, and subsequently picked up an unexplainable mist on my photograph. And on another occasion, and in the same building, a very solid looking ball of light was captured on film, and though invisible to the naked eye, we were aware of a dramatic drop in temperature where the image was taken. I showed these images to a friend, who as a medium, stated that the mist, a pink colour, denoted strong emotions. Another example taken at His Majesty's Theatre by my colleague Duncan Haig showed a white anomaly complete with tail that was captured moving in the bar area, and again, this proved difficult to explain, as it does not fit comfortably with the idea of dust being the cause.

Out of curiosity, I have spent many hours experimenting, creating false 'orbs', by visiting locations where there is an above average amount of dust and debris, and would recommend this to anyone as a means of gauging their images. The simple fact is, there are no definite answers, you can only use your judgement. Another contested phenomenon is the capture of Vortexes on film. Again, due to the sensitivity of modern cameras, Vortexes, thought to be a doorway between the spirit and physical world have been recorded in vast numbers. Unfortunately, many have a rather more mundane explanation, with camera straps or stray hair being put forward as the main culprits. Again however, not all are as easily explained, and there is a strong argument for them being of paranormal origin.

Perhaps the most interesting anomalies are light rods, which appear as streaks of light in motion. These, I would suggest, are a more likely sign of paranormal activity, being far less common than your average 'orb', as they genuinely appear to be moving which suggests purpose. Many images that exist defy logic, but perhaps the most conclusive evidence is the capture of full figure manifestations. A classic example, such as the 'Brown Lady of Raynham Hall' has been seen throughout the world, and still generates argument. Taken in the 1930s, this image, has been thoroughly investigated, and having the sceptical argument of it being tampered with during development ruled out, it remains what many consider to be, the classic ghost photograph. This is the exception rather than the rule, and it's probably realistic to say, that most of us will never capture anything so startling. Despite the many false 'orbs' captured, I still enjoy the experience of recording my visits, and feel it's important to keep a visual record of locations, sometimes, architecturally, proving as interesting as the stories themselves. It is also worth noting that there have been examples recorded of anomalies appearing on photographs, allegedly after processing through spirit intervention.

If you believe that spirit exists, and people continue to live in another form, then it is only natural to assume that they would have retained their personalities. They, like us, would probably not appreciate having demands put on them, and without seeming flippant, would perhaps not want to pose for our cameras. It would appear that any evidence given to us through photography, should be seen as a privilege and not a right. After all, we cannot comprehend how difficult it might be for someone to manifest their energy. We generally cannot see spirit unless it allows us to, and should be aware that as in life here, certain people may be a little camera shy.

The Gelder Bothy

The Gelder Bothy, Gelder stable or Gelder Shiel Stable, take your pick. The name may vary but it is synonymous among walkers and the climbing fraternity, as a place of rugged beauty and mystery. Set high on a wind swept plateau en route to Lochnagar, it is not the most accessible of places, and yet, for the walker, is the only shelter for miles around, and much welcomed. Set in the Balmoral estate, Gelder Bothy was originally the royal stables for Queen Victoria when staying in the adjacent lodge. In the late 1870s, the area was much used by the Royal Family, and she was known to spend long periods of time outside, sketching, while her husband, Prince Albert went off to shoot. The buildings are set upon desolate moor- land, with the only greenery in the vicinity being a small circle of wind-battered trees. On a summer's day the walking is glorious, until the weather takes a turn for the worse, then it can be deadly, as the number of deaths in the area testifies. Rarely written about, its tales are well known among walkers, who have occasionally, been witness to strange and at times frightening events.

I first became aware of the Gelder when in conversation with my friend and colleague, Thane. I mentioned I was gathering information on supernatural tales connected to Aberdeen and we talked at some length about the diverse locations I had heard of, if not visited. He said, it was a pity I was not writing about the shire, as he had a frightening experience on the Balmoral estate some years ago. He was convinced as to its authenticity, and it was this story that persuaded me to 'cast the net wider'. Thane and his two companions, had spent the day walking in the area, and were tired by the time they arrived at the Gelder Bothy. Upon entering, they discovered that there were a number of wooden cot beds in the room, two on one side with another two opposite. The single room had a table and some benches in it, but very little else in the way of furniture. Though, he surmised, if you have ever done a hard days walking, you will appreciate that even the most basic of surroundings can be a Godsend. I was told, the lodge opposite is much more salubrious, however this is kept locked and secure at all times, until the Royal Family wish to use it. So the Gelder it was.

After eating and catching up on the day's events, and as there was no electricity available in the building, it made sense to have an early night. They were soon asleep. Thane, not sure of the time, was rudely awoken by the following: "It must have been the middle of the night I woke, feeling terrified as I heard a loud groaning coming from the centre of the room. I was too scared to shout out to my friends who were sleeping at the other side of the room. The groaning sound went on for what seemed 20 minutes, then, it stopped. In the morning I asked my friends if they had heard it, one did, the other didn't." The friend who had heard the noise said, that he too, was terrified by the noise, and could not explain it's source. They discussed the possibility of it being a stag outside, but no, both were in agreement, it came from the centre of the room. They left and continued their walking but could not shake of the events of the previous night, so much so in fact that when they got home, they asked the wife of the friend, who had slept through it all if he made strange noises in his sleep? They were both pretty certain, that it was almost definitely not him, but needed further confirmation. They were told that he didn't snore. Thane had heard stories about the Gelder previously, about the unexplained noises, and the reports of people seeing faces at the window, peering in, but had never given it much thought. He approached his father Brian, a keen climber in his time, who verified the fact, that the place was well known among walkers, and how strange incidents were reported periodically.

I was very keen to find out more and decided to have a look in the library for more information, and though there have been many good books written about the area from a mountaineer's point of view, there was very little on the history of the Gelder itself. One interesting aside, I discovered, concerned the tale of two men, woken in the night by a scraping at the door, and after plucking up the courage to investigate, witnessed a deer running off which though probably alarming at the time does, not qualify as 'ghost story'. Wanting to know more, I contacted a local climber through an enquiry posted onto a mountaineering web site. I wanted more background information on the area and was pleased to receive a prompt reply from Derek who wrote the following. 'A mutual friend of ours, Mike, who is unfortunately now dead, once told me that he and two pals spent a night in the Gelder in Winter (this was in the days before the bunks were installed, only planks nailed on to the rafters, and space for four with a ladder for access.) He said that they were awakened by a continuous hammering on the door and couldn't understand why the person didn't come in because the snib was on the outside of the door. When Mike climbed down the ladder to open the door, the noise stopped. He opened the door to find no one there. But the strange thing about this was that a lot of snow had fallen that evening and there were no footprints on the doorstep.' He stated: "I knew Mike very well like Brian (Thane's dad) and he was not the type to make up stuff like that." I spoke to Thane about this, retelling the tale, and was interested to learn that there were rumours that someone had died in a storm near the Gelder; though no one was quite sure when this had taken place.

I decided to speak to Derek about this and was surprised by his speedy reply, which arrived the same day, it read; 'It is certainly true that a walker coming down from Lochnagar in very bad weather tried to enter the Gelder stable, but it was locked. He did in fact die on the doorstep. I think it was around 1948. Apparently when the King, George V1, heard about it he told the Balmoral estate factor that the stable should be left open at all times. Thereafter, the stable was used at weekends by climbers and then became known as the Gelder Bothy.' He went on to say that: "I have also been fascinated by the tales associated with the place and have made a point of staying there alone on several occasions, out of curiosity, but had no strange experiences, but there are some people who claim they have." I was greatly intrigued by the story especially as the climber had perished in winter- time, the same season both Mike and Thane's experiences took place. The tragic events surrounding the climber's passing may be instrumental in his re appearances in the winter months, and would appear to be a replay of events from the past. A passing such as this, in my opinion is likely to leave strong emotions in the residual energy of the area, which is unlikely to ever change.

A North East Storage Facility

Due to the sensitive nature of the location of this building and of its purpose I have been obliged to change the names of those involved. As you will see the details of the exact location of the building has deliberately been kept vague however, despite this, the facts of the case are true. The location in question lies approximately 20 miles west of Aberdeen and is situated in a quiet rural village popular with tourists due to its proximity to an important heritage trail. The storage depot in question, built in 2002, is on the site of a former store which belonged to the railway as did the surrounding land. Old maps suggest there were a number of other buildings in close proximity to the current store. These buildings according to the map comprised of a smithy and a lodge, this may have belonged to the nearby estate. Records show that the area at the time was used mainly as farmland and though there has been significant developments in the area of recent years there is still huge tracts of unspoiled land nearby. The storage facility, which as mentioned was built fairly recently is an innocuous looking building and like many modern buildings of its kind seems at odds with the pleasant green of its surroundings. The interior consists of a labyrinth of corridors with workshops and storerooms running of them and given the modernity of the surroundings you would find it hard to believe how it could possibly be the setting for alleged poltergeist activity, but you would be wrong.

The activity was not noticeable when the first employees moved in, perhaps things were happening in an imperceptible manner or some physical intervention was a catalyst for the increase in paranormal activity. All that is known is that in 2005 strange things began to happen, allegedly strange enough to warrant the depot manager seeking help from the church to perform a clearance and blessing. The first indications of activity began almost imperceptibly when staff began to notice the atmosphere in certain parts of the building beginning to feel oppressive and heavy particularly in two of the upstairs storerooms. Staff were known to dislike working there and would feel unsettled whenever they had to conduct their duties in that area. Coupled with the fact that objects appeared to be moved in the area and in some of the nearby offices the events became the subject of hushed conversations. Given the modernity of the workplace no one could understand why a spirit, if that's what it was, would be present there and subsequent research on the immediate area did not point to anything untoward, no battles fought or burial grounds in the vicinity only farmland. This was not to say that everyone immediately jumped to the conclusion that there was spirit activity in the building, some of the more sceptically inclined staff felt that it was more than likely the product of overactive imaginations. Despite this, a previous manager felt so strongly about the situation that he apparently took the unusual step of having the area blessed and though appearing to work for some time only quelled the activity for a short time.

Having known someone who worked there I was put in touch with the owner of the depot who agreed to let me visit to take some photographs and have a look around. I arrived on a cold and bright morning and the first thing that I noticed was the fact that the surroundings were completely innocuous and not at all the kind of place that typifies a 'haunted house'. Part of the enjoyment of visiting haunted locations is the historic buildings themselves and having the opportunity to look round them immersing oneself in their history however on this occasion the building was brand new and as you would imagine made from nondescript materials, stone block and plastic. Despite the mundane surroundings I remained focussed and was taken along to the storage area where the alleged activity was noted to be most prevalent and turning the corner was faced with a long white corridor. I walked to the end of the corridor which was dully lit and instantly became aware of a strong presence which appeared to linger in front of the store room door. I was told later that this was where most people had experienced a change in atmosphere and temperature. I remained standing in the corner for around a minute until the feeling went and though not frightening it still felt a little oppressive. I was then shown into the storeroom where again the same uneasy sensation came over me, particularly at one end of the room where a number of large storage cabinets stood and again like before the feeling dissipated fairly quickly.

The first impression I got was that of a male energy and I was curious as to why someone's spirit would be attached to these surroundings even in visitation, they seemed so bland, however I quickly checked myself as it is common knowledge that many spirit people attach themselves to areas where there has been a connection to them in the past.

I left after taking more images though nothing unusual appeared on any of the photographs and decided to try and find out more about the location. After an initial search I drew a blank and could find no clue as to who this person was, after all the building was new and there had certainly been no deaths recorded on the premises since its opening. Perhaps it was someone who had worked the land before any of the surrounding buildings went up, someone connected to the old estate though checking this proved an impossible task and I was left frustrated by my lack of success.

I contacted the depot some time later and as luck would have it had the opportunity to speak to three members of staff who provided me with some very interesting information. Although there was still a pervasive atmosphere in certain areas of the building events had begun to take a more dramatic turn. It was in the Autumn of 2006 that a sudden burst of spirit activity occurred which made staff in no doubt as to what was causing the strange atmosphere. It was mid morning and John who was working opposite the staff room was taken by surprise as 'two almighty crashes' sounded behind him and fearing something had happened to a colleague 'leapt up and went straight to the staff room, to find the door was closed and the lights were out'. On switching on the light, John was surprised to see the wall clock had been knocked from the wall and was sitting upright against the opposite wall with the number twelve showing on its face. Even more perplexing was the fact that; "All the papers on the notice board were scattered on the other side of the room but all the pins were still in the board." Despite it being around break time there was no one else in the area and feeling alarmed John left the room and returned to his workspace where he waited for his colleagues. Later, in conversation with others it was found that no one else in the building had heard anything.

John was not reassured when a few days later his colleague, Ray asked him into his office where sitting on the floor was a neat pile of crumpled paper sitting in a perfect circle. The bin had been upended and the paper left 'like a sandcastle when you lift off the bucket'. The door had been locked all night and there was no explanation as to how the paper had ended up this way. John was surprised to hear his colleague remark: "The poltergeist has struck again, then!" When pressed to elaborate Ray explained that there had been paranormal activity in the building some time ago which no one could explain and his line manager at the time had the building exorcised. The current manager on being approached reiterated this though was reluctant to provide further comment.

Despite the blessing staff are still only too aware of the ongoing activity though it must be said nothing quite as dramatic as the objects being moved in the staff room has been noted of late. Some staff however are unhappy to be left alone in certain parts of the building with the two stores upstairs remaining unpopular to work in. It is in this area that the cleaner has stated that she has seen 'grey people' and so serious she is in her conviction that she refuses to work in this area. I can concur that this area retains an unusual atmosphere especially the aforementioned corridor where I was acutely aware of a presence during my first visit. Despite a pervading sense of unease among staff and a palpable sense of expectation things quietened down with nothing out of the ordinary being reported until October 2007 when I was contacted by employee Joan who described the following: "I was coming out of the store and facing down the corridor when I saw a small dark figure male figure through the glass panels of the fire doors, when I kept walking towards him he moved away and appeared to go down the stairs, I went through the door to find the stairs empty and subsequently no one else in that part of the building." It was not till later that she realised she may have possibly seen a ghost though at the time did not feel particularly afraid.

Staff have commented that these occurrences though unnerving only happen on occasion and due to their sporadic nature the atmosphere is generally peaceful however a recent incident highlights the fact that the presence is never far away. A few short weeks after the figure was sighted in the top stairwell staff began complaining that the lift was playing up. As moving large objects to the upper stores is an integral part of the job it was not long before an engineer was called out to look at the problem. The engineer stayed for some time and finding no fault was perplexed as to why the lift kept ascending to the top floor when there was no one there. Despite numerous tests nothing untoward was found and when leaving commented that the lift appeared to be sensing someone that was not there as this was the only explanation as to its behaviour. He knew nothing of the stories attached to the store and left after the lift appeared to be functioning normally again. To this day no one can explain why this problem occurred though periodically it 'plays up'.

It was around this time that I had the good fortune to have the following information passed on to me. I was told that one of the cleaning staff, Lorraine is particularly sensitive to spirit and though seen as a gift it has on occasion driven her to distraction, being interrupted in her work by the sudden appearance of spirit people. This is particularly true of the depot where prior to the blessing a 'male in uniform' was apt to make himself known. He was described as wearing a uniform not dissimilar to that of the Royal Air Force though by her own admission she was not certain if it was. She did not get the best feeling from him and described in some detail to my colleague that she first became aware of his presence by the sudden manifestation of unexplained odours. These include the smell of 'rotten neeps' which to her has indicated someone unpleasant or 'nae good' in the vicinity and at other times perfume or tobacco. Unfortunately it was the former that heralded his appearances causing her to be unwilling to linger in either the East or West store. For whatever reason, the spirit was attracted to these areas in particular and would play tricks on Lorraine by constantly switching of her vacuum cleaner prompting her at one point to shout: "If you want peace just let me get on with it and I will be out of your way!" This apparently worked. Lorraine also described seeing shadows 'running along the walls' in the stores and would find, much to her annoyance, the occasional dustbin thrown into the corridor after cleaning the area. It was this accumulation of events that prompted the store manager to seek help from the church and despite the blessing she still does not enjoy working on her own and is apt to get the task done quickly.

In conclusion one could argue that the 'technical problems' concerning the lift for example, is just that, rather than anything untoward though it is only when there is no rational explanation apparent that one should look further as much here defies logic. What has caused and is still causing this activity is uncertain though even the most sceptical of staff are wavering in their convictions when it comes to objects being moved and figures being glimpsed. The building itself offers no clues as to who has is causing this other than perhaps it is someone who lived or worked on the site when it belonged to the railway, perhaps some tragedy did occur in the mists of time. The other alternative theory is perhaps the objects in the store themselves act as a magnet for the unknown visitor as the building contains examples of historic farm machinery. The case is open to interpretation though certain staff now bid their unseen visitor a 'good morning' when entering the reputedly haunted area and it appears to have lightened the atmosphere.

Constitution Street

The story was told to me recently by Eileen Clark who I met at a local history group. This story like so many others involved a visitation that was not alarming but rather life changing in its most positive sense, providing great evidence for the person involved of continuing life. The witness to this event was Eileen's grandmother and took place many years in the early 1900's at 64 Constitution street Aberdeen. What is most fascinating about the following is it involved the spirit of one of Aberdeen's most respected historical figures that of Priest Gordon.

Charles Gordon was born in 1772 the youngest of nine children, he studied for the priesthood in France but was forced to leave due to the outbreak of the revolution returning to Aberdeen. He continued his studies until 1795 when he was ordained into the priesthood. By all accounts acts of kindness came naturally to Charles Gordon a fact that did not go unnoticed among the people of the city, Catholic or not his love of humanity rose above all. He was described as what we would call being down to earth and seemed to posses a missionary zeal in his work in the most positive sense. This was exemplified by his work undertaken with the cities poor which in the early 1800's were manifold. There was no social services or pensions in place to help the hungry and homeless and it was only the tireless work of people like Charles Gordon that could mean the difference between life and death for the most vulnerable. His ecclesiastical duties were varied and interesting, working in the soup kitchen in Loch Street, building orphanages for the many destitute children of that time and performing many other charitable acts.

In later life an ambition long harboured by Charles Gordon came to fruition with the founding of St. Peters Roman Catholic school in Constitution Street. The school had two wings added to it to act as orphanages for the children of his congregation and provided much needed security for many. It was in the building adjacent to the school that he spent his remaining years until his passing on the 24th November 1855.

At the time of his death the public outpourings of grief were unprecedented with thousands lining the street to pay tribute including the Lord Provost and many other dignitaries. It should also be noted that as a measure of his popularity his passing brought together those from many different denominations to mourn him. The Aberdeen Journal of the time wrote 'he took particular interest in the young and in educating and providing for them supplying to many the place of a parent'. The funeral procession passed along King Street with his congregation taking turns to bear the coffin to his final resting place in the Snow Churchyard, Old Aberdeen. Though he himself had passed, his work continued and to commemorate his life and achievements a statue was commissioned in 1859 which was sculpted by Alexander Brodie. The statue was placed outside the school which relocated to Nelson Street where it remained for many years before both school and statue were relocated to King Street. The building then became used for a number of different purposes, housing, a Polish club and the 'Shiprow Tavern' which was a voluntary group providing food for homeless men which I cant help thinking Charles Gordon would have approved of.

It was in the early1900's that this particular story took place in the former home of Priest Gordon. Eileen takes up the story: "Grandmother woke up and was immediately aware of the smell of pipe tobacco being smoked, she sat up in her box bed and saw a figure sitting in an armchair at the fireside, smoking his pipe, the time of the occurrence was the middle of the night." Her grandmother went on to say she did not feel afraid but: "Was shocked," at the occurrence, saying that it convinced her of, "Life after death," which apparently was not a subject she talked about very much. The figure was described as 'very distinct but of a slightly less than solid state, smoky but not see through, he was dressed in priests robes, sitting in an armchair smoking a pipe. He did not speak or acknowledge my grandmother. He remained visible for a sufficient length of time for grandmother to become aware the figure was that of father Gordon.'

Eileen then went on to state that: "My grandmother was a schoolteacher and was never anything other than a very down to earth person. She was a Catholic and the subject of ghosts, paranormal activities would have been very much of a taboo subject hence her reluctance to relate her story to other than a few. I believed her implicitly as she was never given to flights of the imagination."

I was very impressed with this story given that it was told to Eileen many years ago by her grandmother when she in her youth, it amazed me how vivid the details were like it had happened only yesterday and more than suggests its authenticity. As far as I am aware this was a one off incident or at least the only one witnessed, but was it a replay of father Gordon or was he in actual visitation enjoying a pipe by his fireside, returning to somewhere he loved? There is no definitive answer as it all comes down to belief, personally I would like to think that he had come back in to our atmosphere to relive a peaceful moment or two. Factually, all we do know is that he passed over some 45 years previous to the sighting and this was the house he had stayed in. The old school today, after lying empty for many years, is now a home for the elderly and has thankfully retained its grand exterior though like so many streets in the area Constitution Street is only a shadow of its former self having suffered at the hands of the developers like so many others.

Kaimhill Primary School

An unusual series of events were brought to my attention concerning the relatively modern building that is Kaimhill Primary School. The school, originally a secondary was built, in 1951 and used as such until 1971 before becoming a primary school. Sightings of a figure have been reported in recent years, however there is little to suggest what has caused this manifestation. There are a number of possible causes for the activity; however this is purely conjecture on my part at present. Before cutting to the chase it is worth taking a look at the area which up until relatively recent times had been open countryside. Historically the Garthdee/Kaimhill area would have consisted of the odd farmhouse and little else. The only major incident of note in the area is that of the battle of 'Two Mile Cross' which took place in 1644 during the Scottish Civil War. The battle took place roughly where the current retail park at the Bridge of Dee sits, between the Royalist army led by Lord Montrose and the Covenanter forces of Lord Burleigh. The Royalist forces consisted of Irish infantry and Highland Scots and despite the overwhelming numbers of Lord Burleigh,s Aberdeen garrison the battle went ahead. In 1644, as you can imagine, Aberdeen was considerably smaller and with the site of the battle being in open countryside it left the Covenanters with a fairly long march ahead as they went to meet their opponents. The battle was short and victory for the Royalist army came quickly. Despite the fierce fighting casualties were relatively light on both sides with the defeated army losing only 160 men. In the aftermath of the battle there was no mercy shown for the people of Aberdeen and the neighbouring towns and villages, indeed the whole area was subjected to widespread looting. Despite the area having a bloody past, the figure witnessed is regarded as female and although it might be easier to suggest she had some connection with the only incident of historic note in the area I am unconvinced. Kaimhill itself became a market garden consisting of 135 acres in the early 19th century and a number of farms sprang up and remained thus until the encroachment of the developing scheme in the mid 20th century.

I am personally more drawn to another theory though, I might add, not wholly convinced. I have perhaps been slightly misleading when I mentioned there had been only one incident of note in the area, as the following testifies. Though not of the same magnitude as the battle of 'Two Mile Cross', it is still an interesting, albeit grim, chapter in recent history which many Aberdonians may well know of. The incident to which I refer is the 'Coffin Lids Case' of 1944. The setting for the incident was Kaimhill crematorium and involved the managing director, James Dewar and undertaker Alick George Forbes. The pair had concocted a scheme well ahead of its time when they undertook a programme of recycling. However what they were recycling was coffin lids which were removed prior to cremation and turned into an array of household goods by various employees. This was enough to cause public upset but the discovery of unrelated bodies being cremated together and the possible removal of personal effects sent the local population into a frenzy, so much so that the trial took place in Edinburgh. James Dewar was found guilty of the theft of one thousand and forty-four coffin lids and sentenced to three years imprisonment while Forbes was charged with the reset of one hundred lids and sentenced to six months. This may have no bearing on the sightings at Kaimhill Primary School. However the theory of a disgruntled spirit wandering the area restlessly is certainly worth considering.

The following account was provided by Mrs.Jean Horne who has lived locally for many years and knows the area well. She is at a loss to explain why a spirit should be present in the school other than it may have had some historic connection to the area but never the less has been witness to a number disturbing incidents. Mrs. Horne, who works as a cleaner at the school, provided the following accounts which were all experienced first hand, by her and her colleagues. It was in April approximately two years ago that she first saw the mysterious figure while working and explained the following: "I was cleaning the stairs at the far end of the building beside classrooms six and seven when I felt as if I was being watched and on looking up to the top landing I saw this black veiled face looking down, it immediately drew back behind a wooden board." She was, alarmed as you can imagine, and left the area after being overcome with a 'chilling sensation'.

Some days later she approached her supervisor and another colleague, whose job it is to clean the top floor of the building, and though reticent at first recounted her tale. Her supervisor turned out to have experienced exactly the same scenario with the circumstances being identical down to the time of day, in the afternoon between three and five. Her colleague went on to describe how she always felt a presence in room seven and did not like cleaning there on her own. It was only after her own experience that she became aware of how many other people had seen something of the same description, always a head looking round the corner of the stair wearing what appeared to be a black veil. It was with a sense of trepidation that the work was now carried out with the staff trying not to linger too long in that area.

Not long after this another peculiar incident occurred, but this time in a different location. The same peculiar feelings were now being sensed in the back gym, situated at the other end of the building. Despite being a topic of great discussion no one could rationalise why the figure would be there and in turn who it was. The activity stepped up a notch when one afternoon the supervisor was working in the red corridor, which runs parallel to the gym hall and the garden. As she was standing there she became aware of footsteps coming up behind her and thinking it was a co-worker turned to speak only to find the corridor empty. Frightened she quickly went to find her colleague who insisted that at no time was she in the area.

Jean continues to clean at the school and although she has not seen the figure for the last eight to nine months is still wary of its presence, as are her colleagues. She has spent some considerable time reading books on the area but so far has not been able to ascertain what was on the site of the school. Out of interest she contacted a previous supervisor at the school who spoke about a 'grey lady' though she could not elaborate on this. Another cleaner who wished to remain anonymous reported similar feelings, extreme temperature drops in the corridor and an eerie feeling while in the gym hall. Though she is unsure of its origin she has felt scared on occasion and could offer no rational explanation for her feelings. During my research I discovered some old maps that clearly show a building called Kaimhill Farm on the site of the current school. The building was in existence on a 1909 map and in others up until the 1950s when it appears to have been demolished to make way for school. Perhaps then, someone with a connection to the farm is the most likely suspect.

North Silver Street

Set back from Golden Square, North Silver Street is now a fairly congested road. With many businesses in the area and the resultant parking issues it is far busier than in 1980 where this story took place. The former house, now flats, still stands near Ruby Place, though according to one of the former occupants it is far more salubrious now than when he lived there, sharing one of the flats with five others. The flat at the time was cramped, especially since there were five student occupants residing, and with the toilets on the landing still in use it was not the most comfortable of surroundings.

The house itself, for it had been a fashionable abode at one time, had been the home to a succession of relatively wealthy Aberdonians, as had many of its neighbours. Set back from Union Street and at one time boasting a small garden in Golden Square it was a respectable area in the early parts of the 19th century where residents enjoyed a certain amount of peace and quiet away from the burgeoning development of the main thoroughfare. Notable owners from 1850 included the Reverend Primrose, Thomas Primrose, advocate and a Miss Gibson with the building's use in 1895 being described as Artillery Volunteer Orderly Rooms. As the 19th century gave way to the 20th the need for increased housing stock became apparent and many of the once grand dwellings were converted into flats changing the look and social order of areas such as North Silver Street forever. The only further change of note at this time was the founding of a dance school in the building known as Donald's Dancing Academy with James F. Donald first appearing in 1910 with the name continuing into the 1950s.

As Mark pointed out, students being students their flat was something of an open house which at first was fun but soon began to get on the nerves of some of the residents who were trying to hold down jobs to supplement their meagre grants. Given that their neighbours were also 'studying' the constant movement of those staying up late to burn the midnight oil in the block began to manifest itself in arguments. The peculiar layout of the flat played its part in the increasingly volatile situation being that a number of rooms could only be accessed by others making privacy a distant memory. To this day, Mark, is in two minds whether the constant stream of visitors did not play its part in the strange 'vibe' apparent in the flat. During our meeting he admitted that there were many tensions playing out between the tenants who were often 'under each other's feet' and visitors who would turn up unannounced caused arguments between the tenants.

The first indication that something unusual was taking place was when Mark was 'accused' of standing at the foot of the bed of one of the female students early one morning 'grinning at her', an accusation he flatly denied. The fact that he had not been in the building at the time, later confirmed by his girlfriend, did nothing to persuade their flat mate otherwise. She remained adamant that he had been present in her room, watching her and began to look on him with suspicion. This further soured the already strained relationships within the flat and after confiding in his girlfriend they decided that the flat mate was either delusional or had dreamt it, trying their best to put it behind them.

It was not long after that Mark and Susan, on arriving home, were pulled aside by another tenant who stated that on passing their room they noticed that the door was ajar and from within the blackness they heard a 'soft chuckling and mumbling'. It was with some trepidation that they entered room which was jokingly referred to as the 'tomb'. The 'tomb' derived its name from the fact that it did not contain any widows and without natural light was constantly in utter darkness unless of course illuminated by the single light inside. After receiving this information the couple became increasingly paranoid about spending any time in their room, which they began to avoid if alone. It soon became apparent that whatever was going on had succeeded in cranking up the tension to the point where people did not like being in the building on their own, especially as voices could still be heard on occasion inside the dark and empty bedroom. Mark admitted that people were too scared to visit the bathroom at night unless accompanied as it involved a torturous journey up the communal stairway where in the cold light of early morning imaginations ran wild. Strange cold spots began to appear and again the sound of laughter could be heard on occasion from the 'tomb'.

Given the lack of money available to upgrade their accommodation the group decided to 'hang in there' till the lease expired and try and make the best of an unfavourable situation. This included taking over some of the 'better' rooms when given the opportunity which particularly appealed to Mark and Susan who were loathe to spend any time in their room. One such opportunity arrived when circumstance dictated that there would only be the two of them in the building one night. Given that the living room was the coziest in the house, Mark and Susan decided to drag their mattress through to watch television from the comfort of their bed. The evening passed uneventfully and eventually in the early hours they decided to call it a night. It was very late and as the room was quiet sleep soon followed. Mark does not recall what the time was when he first became aware of Susan murmuring in her sleep, but he was immediately awake. He lay awake in the gloom as the murmuring became words and his partner could plainly be heard talking in her sleep and sounding more frantic with each passing second. Mark propped himself up as Susan tossed and turned next to him and as she woke in fright they were both transfixed by the sight of a 'grey mist like a dry ice machine' floating in the corner of the room. They clung to each other as the mist remained in the air slowly moving though it never 'formed a discernible shape'. They lay, propped up and in a state of alarm, for around 30 seconds before the mist evaporated and they dove for the light switch. Lying in the newly illuminated room all was as normal except that Susan became aware of sudden pain along her back. Sitting up fully a number of red welts were noticed running across her back and it was at this point that she described in a shaking voice the terrible dream she had in which a monkey sat on her shoulders hampering her breathing and scratching her. The couple did not sleep for the rest of the night and though thankfully the incident was never repeated, they never used the living room again. Not long after the first of the flat mates moved on prompting the others to look for their own flats. It was at this point Mark and Susan also left and it was with no small amount of relief that they left North Silver Street behind. The flat has since been upgraded and sold on to private owners.

Mark was at pains to point out that when he stayed there the building was considerably more ramshackle as were many others on the street. The surrounding buildings have also undergone a number of changes including the former bingo hall, now also gone, leaving a bricked up door to mark the spot. During our conversation he put forward the theory that perhaps the bad atmosphere was in some way a symptom of having a constant stream of disparate people through the door. The source of the voices in his room remains unexplained, as does the strange mist but he conceded that perhaps Susan had scratched herself in her sleep during a particularly vivid nightmare. Despite this, he could think of nothing that would explain the thick white fog in the corner of the room and the feeling of dread that they felt in its presence.

This story is open to interpretation though I personally feel that an atmosphere conducive to creating a physical manifestation can be caused by people's state of mind and interactions. As with most old buildings there was possibly something in the residual energy of the building already and all it took was the right combination to unlock it.

First Bus King Street

Perhaps the most frustrating search I have ever undertaken relates to one of Aberdeen's most widely known 'ghost stories', concerning the still wandering spirit, of Captain Beaton of the Gordon Highlanders. There have been numerous articles on this particular haunting though the most substantial evidence relating to his actual existence, such as his full name, birth and death date still manages to elude everyone. One reason, facts are hard to find is probably down to the supposed nature of his passing and of the social climate during the inter- war years in Edwardian Britain. I have spent countless hours trying to build up a picture of the tragic circumstances surrounding the case and have still arrived at more questions than answers, and despite numerous searches through the appropriate public records, I consider this a work in progress.

The King Street bus depot itself, has undergone numerous changes in its long history, from army barracks to tram depot, and in more recent times, head quarters for the First Bus group. Through all this time, the spectre, metaphorically speaking, of Captain Beaton has been omnipresent, with the first sightings recorded in the early 1920s continuing to the present day where current staff, have claimed to have encountered his presence. The King Street Militia Barracks, as it was known, was built in 1861 housing the Royal Aberdeenshire Highlanders, later to become the 3rd Battalion Gordon Highlanders. Prior to the start of World War One, plans were afoot by Aberdeen Town Council to purchase the site for the development of a tram repair shop, but with the outbreak of the war that same year plans were put on hold. Once again the barracks reverted back to military use becoming home to the Gordon Highlanders. It remained in the hands of the military until the end of the war when in a twist of fate, a massive housing shortage forced the council to convert the King Street building and those adjacent into temporary housing. These abodes, many consisting of single rooms, became home to returning soldiers and their families, and continued to be occupied until 1932 when the residents were eventually re-homed. This allowed the barracks to eventually become the repair shop for trams and buses for which it had been intended, and thus it remained for many years.

The story of Captain Beaton is unusual in that there is a substantial amount of detail of his exploits available in the public domain, yet the lack of hard facts proving his existence are glaringly obvious. The main stumbling block appears to be that of the circumstances surrounding his death, as there is no concrete evidence to back up his passing, most notably a death certificate. Despite this however, I personally feel the stories have a basis in fact, and probably because of the social climate of the times, this evidence has been 'covered up'. Who Captain Beaton was remains shrouded in mystery, and as no one appears to know his first name, it remains highly unlikely that we will ever find out. The Captain,s name however, was most definitely on the lips of the first tenants back in the 1920s, so how did these rumours start?. And what evidence do we really have to verify his existence? The truth is, we have practically nothing concrete to go on, but what we do have are persistent eyewitness accounts that have spanned almost ninety years. So, can they all be imagining it? I personally don't think so. I will tell you the 'facts' of the case as they have been recorded over the years and if I have found anything further to back this up, it has been noted.

It has been recorded in numerous articles over the years that during World War One a Captain with the 3rd Battalion Gordon Highlanders received head injuries in France In 1915, when the regiment was known to have seen action. He was, as many soldiers were, probably treated in France initially at one of the many Red Cross stations before being sent back to Britain to aid recuperation. Hospitals at the time were unable to cope with the vast numbers of injured men and staff were therefore forced to utilise other buildings, turning them into temporary hospitals. Aberdeen had, like many other cities, examples of these temporary hospitals, and it was to the music rooms at the High School for Girls (now Harlaw Academy) that he allegedly returned in 1915.

In response to this first piece of information I contacted the Academy's librarian, who suggested I speak to Aberdeen City Council archives on the matter, as their records of the period were sporadic. After a short search they were able to locate a set of school magazines from 1915 which had the headmistress' report inside. This detailed the school's usage at that time though the entry itself was described as 'frustratingly brief'. The headmistress recorded that the school buildings were taken over as the headquarters of the 1st Scottish General Hospital with pupils being moved out to alternative accommodation. The injured men were apparently housed in the music rooms, though again, there was no evidence of a Captain Beaton being there.

I have read two differing accounts of what happened next. The first states that he was sent to the military hospital at the King Street Barracks to recuperate, circumventing the High School for Girls. The second, a conflicting story, suggests he first went to the High School before being sent back to the King Street Barracks for more long term care. Which is true, if either, remains a mystery. Incidentally, the military hospital at the King Street Barracks is still standing today, used partially for storage though the higher floors have stood empty for many years. The old hospital can still be accessed through the repair shop, a later addition to the building. The hospital itself is eerie, desolate, and not very pleasant, the floor now littered with the skeletons of dead pigeons and their accumulated excrement are testament to its dereliction, as is the antique bus memorabilia now caked in a thick layer of dust. It doesn't take much imagination to see that it must have been a very depressing place even when in use as a hospital. There appears to be very little natural light and the flaking grey paint, which I suspect is original to the period, does little to illuminate the rooms.

The next time Captain Beaton's name crops up is in 1918 when it was written that he was due to be posted back to France. Apparently not able to face the prospect and having no doubt already seen too much, the unfortunate Captain took his own life by hanging himself in the south turret, which in 1918 was part of the officers' mess. The body was discovered the next morning and cut down. This is where things become complicated. Suicide at that time was considered a 'crime' and frowned upon by both the church and society as a whole. In fact, in less enlightened times, before the events of 1918, it has been recorded that the bodies of suicides would be publicly hanged as a 'punishment', a practice both barbaric and absurd. The very fact that society could not comprehend why someone should commit this act is a measure of their lack of empathy towards those deeply troubled. This is illustrated by the fate of many returning soldiers during this period, when the number of suicides rose dramatically. It is in all probability due to the nature of his passing, that I have been unable to find out the exact details of the case. His death certificate, despite searching both locally and nationally, remains elusive and one can only speculate as to its fate. There are a number of theories that could account for this. In those circumstances the local fiscal would hold records of 'sudden' death and would normally destroy records after a period of time. Equally likely is that truth may have been 'hushed up' so as not to affect morale among the troops. As was common practice at that time, many suicides would be interred in an unmarked grave, further clouding the search for the truth. I did discover however, one Beaton, buried in St.Machar churchyard, Old Aberdeen, though no name, indeed no stone to put a name on exists.

The war ended shortly after his death and eventually, due to the housing shortage, the Barracks were decommissioned and the families moved in. It was around this period that rumours began to circulate about the shadowy figure of a soldier in uniform seen in and around the building. Despite this, it took almost eighty years before two former residents of the Barracks, Mrs May Cooper and Mrs Helen Leiper both contributed to articles in both the 'Leopard Magazine' and the 'This Is North Scotland' forum respectively and it became public knowledge. The articles themselves are fascinating, providing a snapshot of Aberdeen life in the 1920s and of the hardships faced by families in the post war years. Both witnesses, young children at the time, had heard rumours of a ghost, with Mrs. Cooper stating that people began to hear strange noises, while others complained of cold spots in certain parts of the building, though neither knew that something far more tangible was about to take place. In the article Helen explained that during a visit from family friends the adults were chatting and, feeling left out and bored, she wandered upstairs. While on the top floor she came across a room with a cot bed in it and on the bed sat a soldier wrapping a bandage round his hand, wearing a khaki uniform. The soldier rose and vanished leaving Mrs.Leiper looking at the empty cot. She told the adults who assumed she had imagined it. It wasn't till many years later when bus drivers reported seeing the figure of a soldier at the depot that she felt vindicated and realised that what she witnessed all those years ago was real.

The name Beaton was off the radar as far as any published accounts go until the 1970s when a string of unexplained events made the then current crop of employees unwilling to be alone in certain parts of the building. Unsurprisingly the activity was particularly prevalent in the vicinity of the former officer's mess, now the staff canteen. The papers ran a number of articles at the time in which drivers reported having felt cold air blown on their necks while eating alone, being touched and in one well documented case a driver seeing a figure in a kilt walking up the stairs in front of him. This particular staircase appeared to be at the centre of much of the activity and the toilets, which used to exist on the top landing, were considered a no-go area for many, with doors opening and closing while there was no one there. In more recent times incidents of a figure seen walking through a wall, where apparently a doorway used to be, have also been reported. This fact was verified by a current employee, John, who on showing me round the building recounted the tale, stating that during building work in the 1980s, the original doorway was blocked off and ever since then a shadowy figure has been seen walking through the wall occasionally.

Having been aware of this tale since a child I was very keen to look round the former barracks and had the opportunity to do so in 2006 as part of a local history project I was facilitating. During the tour I was able to visit the area that used to house the canteen and before that the officers mess, though since conversion, it apparently bears little resemblance to those rooms. As we walked along the top corridor that runs the length of the King Street building, I became aware that air was noticeably colder than the others we had traversed. A number of large heaters lined the corridor which when touched were roasting hot, surprisingly though, the air remained cool. The building, I was told, had changed a number of times since the 1970s and though still atmospheric in part, has essentially a new interior. It was hard to imagine what it would have looked like when first built, however on the top floor there was still the occasional artifact to remind you of its age.

Perhaps the most interesting and certainly macabre element of my visit was when I was shown around the old officers' mess' now unrecognisable in its modernity. I was directed to a rather nondescript door and handed a torch, puzzled, I was instructed to walk through the doorway and 'shine the torch up wards'. I found myself in the cold grey granite surroundings of the infamous south turret, apparently unchanged since first being built in 1861. I was immediately stuck by how cold it was and looked upwards to see tied to the crossbeams around fifteen feet up, a filthy rope, dirty and frayed which it had obviously at some point been cut through. I was told that this rope had been there since the time of the captain's death and is thought to be the one he used. No one is sure why it still remains there and why it was never removed and if genuine was certainly a grim reminder of past events. On leaving I was taken to the tower at the other side of the building, which in stark contrast had been lined with wood panelling and contained modern office equipment. I subsequently had the opportunity to take some photographs in the turret and garnered some general information on the building, though nothing specific on the haunting. The tour ended and I left at this point.

Four months later I asked permission to return to the barracks and contacted first bus who seemed supportive of my proposal. I arrived with my colleague, Duncan who shares an interest in the history of the barracks. We met first bus employee Jim McDonald who had volunteered to take us round and proved to be an interesting guide with a wealth of knowledge on the depot. Jim had a real interest in local history and his tour provided me with the opportunity to meet staff and hear of their experiences. We first stopped off at the 'officers' mess', took some photographs and again looked inside the turret. Jim mentioned that the corridor we were travelling along was one that footsteps have been heard in when there was no one upstairs and then asked 'if we felt how cold it was'. As before, the temperature was noticeably cooler. We were told, the corridor remains very cold compared to the rest of the building even on the hottest days. Though obviously a natural explanation could be found for this, it still provided food for thought. We went downstairs and passed the spot where the old toilets stood another area that was prone to activity. Jim explained that the most noticeable activity here was the sound of male voices, being heard in conversation and with doors opening and shutting by themselves, the area was usually avoided. He went on to say, for security purposes, these areas were always checked after a reported incident and were always found to be empty.

Continuing on, we met Alexander Leslie, an administration assistant with the company. He pointed out that there was period in the 1970s when things were happening on a regular basis especially to those using the old canteen though it appeared to die down when the building was changed internally. During the refurbishment the canteen was moved to another part of the building with the company boardroom being created. Alexander was aware of a sighting at that time, witnessed by a colleague who described as a 'full figure', having been seen in the company training room formerly the 'old coach trim shop' which is upstairs from the 'running shed', the figure was seen wearing a 'kilt and greatcoat'. Despite his most memorable appearances taking place in the building, his spirit, it appears, is not confined to the inside as became apparent when a female employee working in the coaching office witnessed the following. The employee had been busy in the office when she kept hearing a tapping noise at the window. She turned round to see who was there but was faced with only a 'shadow' which promptly vanished, leaving her in a state of alarm. Alexander went on to say that 'in the evening you do hear taps and different noises, I put it down to pipes cooling down'. He went on to say, that as a sceptic, he felt there was in all probability a natural explanation for many of the reported incidents and with others, he proposed that an over fertile imagination was to blame. During the conversation he went on to say something which I found interesting, that: "In the early reports of sightings a bus driver, Dougie, who was heavily into spiritual things brought a Ouija board down to king Street and got a reading from a captain/corporal Beaton". I found it intriguing that there had been a fallow period of sightings between the 1920s and 1970s and I wondered if the use of the Ouija board in the area had stirred things up. I personally would not use a board having heard too many first hand accounts of people having frightening experiences, but this is down to personal opinion. It was interesting though that the name Beaton came up, suggesting he may have been a corporal instead of a captain, perhaps an other avenue to explore was opening up? After leaving the communications office we were then taken through the old tram shed to the old military hospital to have a look around. It is certainly a gloomy and oppressive place and like before I felt uncomfortable. We took some photographs, and after a while thanked our guide and left.

I had the photographs developed a few days later and noticed that on a number of pictures orbs were present, though I believe that practically all of them can be put down to dust, as the air was thick with it. Despite this however, there was an unusual anomaly in one picture which showed, what appeared to be a large object appearing to contain cells, though again given the amount of debris in the air there could be a mundane explanation.

After the visit, I spent a number of months contacting various agencies such as the Red Cross and the Imperial War Museum to try and find more back ground information on Captain Beaton, even spending hours in the library looking through the Aberdeen Journal, Edwardian Aberdeen's equivalent to the Evening Express, but to know avail .I was told on numerous occasions that without a first name it would be very difficult to find a suitable match and given what little information I have his identity was no nearer to being found. I decided that I would have one more visit to the depot to try and speak to some of the staff who I had not met and collect the questionnaires I had left there previously. I met Jim and was pleasantly surprised when he mentioned that there had been a new incident.

A security worker had been the only person at the depot on Christmas day and was doing a tour of the grounds. He entered the old tram shed and hearing something from the back of the building went to investigate. Thinking someone could have left a radio on by accident he went to locate the source of the noise, which appeared to coming from a locked part of the tram shed. He was stopped in his tracks as he heard two male voices, in conversation coming from inside the old military hospital. The only means of entry to the building is through the tram shed and given it was locked it would have been impossible for anyone to have gained entry. He was somewhat alarmed and left quickly in the realisation, that whatever it was it was best left alone. He recounted the incident to colleagues who came to their own conclusion. After this incident it came to me that I had been blinkered in my search that I had forgotten the possibility that there may be other spirit visitors and given the number of people who lived and died there, soldiers and civilians it was perfectly feasible.

I realised that the evidence I was gathering was purely anecdotal and spent the next few months concentrating on trying to gather concrete facts again to no avail and decided to give myself a break and concentrate on other locations. It was not until August 2006, after deciding to again pay a visit to the depot that I met Dave who works in the main office, co-ordinating bus movements. He told me that many of the workers maintain a healthy scepticism and tend not to jump to conclusions, but explained that a baffling incident happened to a colleague recently, which made him nervous about being alone in the building. He takes up the story: "I was in the depot on my own when someone from accounts, a new start, came by asking to be let in as she had some important work to finish. I found out later she knew nothing of the buildings history. She went upstairs and while in her office heard someone running along the corridor behind her. She thought nothing of it even when the footsteps continued as she sat working in her office. After finishing up, she came downstairs and said to me, before you lock up you had better check if everyone has left, as there is someone moving around up there. I knew there was no one else in, but said nothing, as I didn't want to alarm her. I was very nervous about locking up and did it very quickly." He felt genuinely nervous and stated that small incidents like this happen fairly regularly though staff accept it as part of working there. I have met many employees during my visits and there is a definite split between the sceptics and the more open minded, despite there being overwhelming evidence of spirit activity.

During my many visits there I was impressed by the amount of incidents related to me and I still firmly believe that staff are still experiencing paranormal activity to this day. I am unfortunately no nearer to finding the elusive factual information that I need but put this down to a number of things. Firstly, the idea of a 'cover up' at the time of the war seems plausible and given that a lot of centrally held military records were destroyed in the blitz it is also feasible that Captain Beatons may have been among those. I contacted the Gordon Highlanders museum who kindly searched their records for me, but all that was found was the commerative brochure produced by First Bus which mentions the Beaton story however a retired Major at the museum stated that his: "Name does not appear on the army list of 1914 or

1918." which would indicate he may have been a soldier prior to the outbreak of the war. During this period I was given assistance in searching the "Soldiers who died in the war," database and it became clear that it only holds one at 'home' death during that period for a Beaton though the soldier in question did not die in Aberdeen. Despite this, I am convinced of the authenticity of the sightings but wonder if the spirit person in question is a Captain Beaton, perhaps the name was given inaccurately and it has been someone else all along. Another line of enquiry I hoped to pursue was if he had been in the army before the war then his name may appear on the 1911 census for Aberdeen, giving the barracks as his residential address. Unfortunately however these will not come into the public domain for another five years.

I would dearly love to get to the bottom of this mystery as having a grandfather who served with the Royal Engineers during WW1 I can empathise with the terrible conditions these men had to endure many being barely out of their teenage years at the time. There was no provision for those returning, injured, physically or mentally, no support, basically left to get on with it. In my mind it would be doing "Captain Beaton" a great disservice to not find out who he was while on this earth, to give him a "real name", did he have family? At the very least to have his bravery recognised, in the trenches, while recovering, and to recognise how impossible a task it must have been for him to cope with being recalled to action after his experiences. There are so many unanswered questions, but I would like to believe that given the infrequency of his appearances he is only in visitation, has moved on and has hopefully found some peace.

The South turret, First Bus headquarters, King Street. The alleged
rope from which Captain Beaton took his own life.
(photo: Copyright of the author)

The desolate surroundings of the old military hospital, First Bus, King Street, where voices have been heard by current staff. (Photo: Copyright of the author).

The tragic events leading to the death of Captain Beaton still echoes down the years. (Illustration: Courtesy of Jim Mac Donald)

Commerce Street; scene of with burnings and public executions where the sound of Latin chanting has been heard.
(Photo: Copyright of the author)

The old price list in the cellar of the Moorings Bar, where a disembodied voice demanded its return.
(Photo: Copyright of the author)

Rosemount community centre gym, lights have been switched back on after closing. (Photo: Copyright of the author)

Powis House: Michael Molden demonstrates where he witnessed the sudden appearance of a female spirit. Note the appearance of a large Orb (Photo: Copyright of the author)

Michael Molden photographed a few seconds later as the temperature dropped and Orb intensified. (Photo: Copyright of the author)

Provost Skenes House, one of Aberdeen's few remaining medieval buildings. Some former residents have found it hard to leave. (Photo: Copyright of the author)

The interior of the old bank, Victoria Court. (Photo: Copyright of the author)

The former workplace of Charles Gordon still stands on Constitution Street. (Photo: Copyright of the author)

The cellar of the old bank where a shadowy figure appeared. Note the very light and fast moving light anomaly at the end of the corridor. (Photo: Copyright of the author)

An ectoplasmic mist caught on camera in the Tolbooth Museum.
(photo: Copyright of the author)

Boddam

The following story is most unusual in that it features what was thought to be an unidentified spirit animal. The circumstances, as you will see, would discount it as being a physical one. To this day they have no idea what caused this activity and to be frank I cannot offer any explanation either. Perhaps there are clues lost in the mists of time that we do not know of but given the scant detail of the house in question's previous owners we are unable to explore this further. It was related to me by my partner's parents who lived at the location of the incident, an old fisherman's cottage in the village of Boddam. The village lies a few miles south of Peterhead, nestling on the rugged cliffs of the East Coast, with its most notable landmark being the Buchaness Lighthouse. The area surveyed by George Stevenson, grandfather of Robert Louis Stevenson, is home to the lighthouse, resting on an outcrop of rock and has helped the local fishing community find safe passage for over 150 years. Though the village has expanded the picturesque cottages of old still provide a charming reminder of the past. Having withstood the battering of the elements for over two hundred years it was in one of those cottages that the incident unfolded.

Valerie and Terry were both stationed at RAF Boddam and had moved into a house in Earls Court, which lay in the village. The building which still stands today, looked entirely different in 1964 both outside and in, having yet to undergo any major refurbishments. The accommodation at that time was described as being 'rough and ready', the décor being old and unchanged for many years. The building also had a number of architectural quirks including an unusual lay out on the top floor. One of these, being a steep, narrow, wooden staircase which led to the loft effectively splitting the top floor in half, leaving a bedroom on either side. The Wright's knew very little about the building's history other than it was likely to have belonged to someone with a seafaring/fishing connection, as were most of the others in the village. They settled in and despite the antiquated surroundings were happily in the process of raising their first daughter when an unexpected and frightening incident came out of the blue and shattered their peace. The house could have an atmosphere and I was told that 'strange things would sometimes happen' including an old clock in the hallway whose components would jangle furiously as if shook by invisible hands. They found this inexplicable rather than frightening and it became a bit of a running joke as Terry would occasionally sneak into the hall to shake the clock, much to the chagrin of his wife. At the top of the stairs lay the two bedrooms and in between, the attic. The stairs were old and narrow and at the top lay a door, which was kept closed at all times, secured by a latch on the outside. Behind the door lay the attic which had no electric light and the one skylight was tiny and black with dirt, providing very little illumination. The family had no real use for the space. It had lain empty for years and contained nothing apart from two old sea chests and a thick carpet of dust. This dust covered the floor liberally and was the accumulation of many years' neglect. It was a perfectly normal night and the family had gone to bed as usual. Settling down they became aware of a series of 'heavy thuds' going across the attic above their heads. They lay awake listening for a while before Terry got up to investigate. The noise stopped abruptly and as he had no torch and noticing the door to the attic was still locked decided to leave further investigation till the morning. In the morning they discovered a baffling and disturbing sight; their white enamel bath had a series of large dusty animal footprints in it as if something had gone into the bath and walked around inside it. Immediately they went up the stairs and looked into the dark attic but hearing nothing and not being able to see into the further recesses decided to leave an investigation till later and locked the door. It preyed on their minds all day, what was it? Where had it come from? And more importantly, how did it get downstairs? These questions were left hanging in the air and it was with some trepidation that the following evening they went to bed. As with the previous night their slumber was broken once more by movement in the attic. A series of thuds as if something was moving around was heard, and again continued for some time before stopping. The next day, as his concern grew Terry approached a friend at the RAF camp and told him of the incidents. His friend was keen to investigate and having borrowed a torch the pair resolved to get some answers. They performed a thorough search of the attic and discovered that the floor, which was deep with dust, was covered in what they described as large animal prints. Despite checking every nook and cranny they found nothing and could not understand how an animal, especially one, which matched the sizeable footprints, would be able to gain access to the loft. After all, the walls were sound and the skylight so rusted they were unable to open it. In desperation, though they inwardly knew it was going to be a fruitless search, they checked the two old sea chests finding nothing other than old clothes. Determined to get to the bottom of the mystery they decided to set a trap to try and catch whatever was making the prints should it return. As the loft stair was so narrow the pair engineered a trap, which could be sprung, should the creature or whatever it was attempt to leave the attic and get to the food which they had now left as bait. The bait had been left sitting precariously on the end of a plank. This would serve a duel purpose, as hopefully, in its attempt to reach the food, it would dislodge the plank causing the animal to fall down the narrow steps whilst an attached pulley would close the attic door trapping it downstairs. If that was not enough then they had also laid three nail beds containing sharpened ten inch nails on the last two steps of the stair and one on the upper hall floor in which they hoped the creature would either be killed or injured. They wanted to be rid of 'it' permanently as they were afraid of what it was capable of doing to their young daughter should it gain access to her room. The size of the prints was also causing concern. They were described as being 'large and not too far off the circumference of a coffee cup'. With the trap set Valerie described how they lay awake that night with her husband 'ready for battle' holding an old bayonet he had found hanging above their bedroom fireplace.

What happened next is something that they will never forget, suddenly from out of nowhere there was a 'terrible commotion and the most terrible sound like a screech' it was described as being an 'unforgettable sound like an animal in great pain'. Terry sprinted from the room to witness the trap sprung, the plank fallen and the door to the attic shut. But there was no sign of anything, living or dead, no blood on the carpet of nails, no fur, just silence. They searched the attic again; the only means of escape a narrow skylight was still shut and so began a restless night's sleep. In the morning they cleared away the trap and waited to see if whatever it was would reappear. But that was it, the noise from the attic stopped as did the unexplained appearance of footprints. From that moment onwards life returned to normal as, eventually, did their sleep patterns. Over forty years have passed since the incident and they still have no answer to the mystery, it remains unexplained. If it had been an animal of flesh and blood, how did it get out of the house when everything was secure? How did it escape injury? They are usually fairly sceptical when it comes to the paranormal but conceded that it seemed the most likely cause of the incident. The building itself has undergone major changes since the time of these events and very little is known of who lived there in the past or what connection, if any, they may have had to the activity. It appears to have been a 'one off' incident but apart from that there is little to go on. The Wright's were posted abroad with the RAF a short while later and though the incident is firmly at the back of their minds these days, when asked they always remember it with great clarity. I can offer no explanation as to these events. I am content to recount the tale, but knowing the family well and their pragmatic nature I believe what they have told me to be the truth. Strange as it may seem, there have been numerous reports of spirit animals sighted throughout history, but what kind of animal could this have been, to have left such large prints, and why was it bound to this house until the chain of events were set in motion and its subsequent departure? We will never know, and possibly just as well.

The Tolbooth

Aberdeen's museum of civic history is one of the city's oldest surviving buildings. The original Tolbooth, a place where council meetings were held and taxes collected, was mostly demolished to make way for the Town House, being built in 1867. The Wardhouse, a place where criminals were held while awaiting trial and part of the original Tolbooth was allowed to remain though now hidden by the newer granite façade. The Wardhouse was completed in 1629 and though it underwent a number of architectural changes, it remained true to its purpose and served as a prison for two hundred years. Today, in its most recent incarnation as civic museum, it is known as the Tolbooth though this is not strictly accurate.

As expected, and given its age, the building has seen many architectural changes over the years, including the relocation of the original entrance from the side of the building to a more prominent position at the front. The side entrance was originally situated up a flight of stairs in what is now known as Lodge Walk. These stairs lead to the overcrowded and unsanitary cells in which many unfortunates spent their last days. This is not to say that most ended their lives at the hands of the city executioner but rather at the whim of the various diseases prolific in such surroundings. For some the small matter of debt could result in their needless death. Death itself did not discriminate between classes and for those languishing in misery it became something of a lottery as to whether they would ever breathe clean air again. Records of the time illustrate this well with up to thirty prisoners, usually debtors, kept at any one time in the cells with little hope of sustenance unless provided for by family, friends or the occasional sympathetic stranger. It is true death was no discriminator between the classes, though the wealthy did have the option of buying a key for the day, allowing them the privilege of respite from the terrible conditions, under the provisio that they returned by nightfall, so their chances of survival were somewhat increased. The least fortunate, those found guilty of the most heinous crimes, and with no hope of remission, also spent their last night on earth there. Kept awake by the sawing of carpenters on the street below as their appointment with the gallows loomed, the idea of a hearty last supper, was unheard of with the rudimentary menu offering only bread and water.

Justice in the 17th century was more often than not swift and brutal and the severity of the punishments meted out far outweighed the crime. The accurate city records are testament to this, and the building would assume the role of holding tank until such times as justice was seen to be done and therefore it is only natural to expect some of these emotions to be stored in the very fabric of the stone work. I first became aware of the Tolbooth through work and subsequently discovered, that like many locals, had walked passed on numerous occasions without realising it was open to the public. I soon began to visit regularly taking along community based groups who had an interest in Aberdeen's past. Needless to say the atmospheric surroundings provided a stark reminder of the conditions faced by those unfortunates and the oppressive feeling in the cells was pervasive as we laboured up the narrow stairways. During my first few visits I did not get any sensations of spirit activity and wondered given its history why it felt so calm. Perhaps I was just there at the wrong time, after all, as in most locations I have visited a lot depends on the conditions, who was with me, the time of day and weather. I came to the conclusion, that given the choice, would you want to continue hanging around, if you forgive the pun, a place that caused such misery? I continued to visit the museum and on a bright winters day in 2006 I had my first taste of what spirit is capable of at the Tolbooth. The tour had gone well and we had assembled in the entrance hall prior to leaving when it was suggested I should take photographs of the group for posterity. The group being new to the city, were happy with this suggestion, especially the children who were having fun vying for their turn. I was then asked if they could use the camera, as it was secure on a tripod I did not see the harm. They took turns to photograph each other and eventually after running out of steam asked if they could take my picture. *At least I could delete it later*, I thought saying: "Snap away." I checked the camera to see how 'bad' it was, being instantly startled by the image of a white mist that had enveloped me. The group began to leave and after promising them copies of the pictures I quickly went to get the image printed. Having an interest in photography I had been trying desperately to capture anything other than the usual orbs for some time, though it ironically took another's hand to do so.

With my interest in the building's possibilities increasing I began to visit the museum as regularly as I could in the hope of capturing the phenomena again but despite my efforts I became disheartened as the images were mostly clear of any anomalies. The atmosphere also remained constant and completely normal and I began to think, perhaps this was a one off. However, this was about to change. In May of 2007 I was assisting a group of adult learners whose interests lay in writing a report on crime and punishment. A tour of the museum was organised as part of the project and having become slightly jaded by the amount of visits undertaken recently I duly arrived. The day was sunny and we started of in the main entrance hall as normal before making our way up to the first floor where there are a number of cells. The group appeared interested and were obviously having fun; things were going well and we ascended the stairs to the condemned cell. The cell in question, unlike the others, has retained its original brick floor and still houses some of the most tangible reminders of our bloody past, including, the blade of the 'maiden' (a precursor to the guillotine), the 'scolds bridle' (a device for stopping women nagging) and various shackles designed to make your last days as uncomfortable as possible. Being one of the smaller rooms in the building, it possesses a particularly oppressive atmosphere, perhaps not helped by the array of sinister devices it holds. In the heat, we stood shoulder to shoulder, rapt, as our guide regaled us with tales of torture.

I stood at the edge of the group who numbering eight were crammed into the small space, when I became aware of an icy cold sensation down my left side accompanied by the shuffling sound of feet on the step leading into the cell. I glanced to my left and saw nothing before turning to my right where I noticed two members of the group looking at me strangely. I looked ahead not wishing to disturb our guide who appeared oblivious to the noise. The noise started up again and I felt as if someone was up close, in my space, a feeling that caused me to me to shiver uncontrollably. Again the sound came but within the cell. I glanced at the group, and now three puzzled and slightly anxious people looked back at me. The sound came again but this time was more akin to a chain being moved. I quickly checked my feet and ruling out the possibility of accidentally moving something I began to feel very uncomfortable. Eventually and thankfully the icy sensations began to dissipate and everything returned to normal. The guide finished and led us from the cell where I whispered: "Did you hear that?" to my colleague, and as she passed whispered: "yes."

Once outside in the welcome sunshine, I spoke to the group who all began to talk excitedly about the strange shuffling noises in the cell. The fact this phenomena was verified by four others, was to me evidence of spirit activity and from that moment I began to look on the building in a different light. My excitement however, was short lived, as subsequent visits yielded next to nothing and I began to believe that whoever was in the cell with us was more likely to have been in visitation rather than someone grounded permanently.

Despite my continuing work related visits things were quiet again until July 2007 when I noticed a paranormal investigation group had organised an overnight vigil in the cells. I quickly jumped at the chance to spend a longer period in the museum and with the promise of things to come I made my way to the building where the excited and possibly slightly nervous group awaited the start of the night's events. After meeting the team running the event we were split into three groups of eight. Each group was given the opportunity to investigate individual cells and allowed the use of various gadgets to record any evidence should it present itself. And so began a long night of ascending and descending the narrow staircases, causing much mock groaning from the participants. The most interesting area on the first floor, as it transpired, turned out to be the 'civic' room. This room, not originally part of the building was built at a much later date above the arch in Lodge walk and houses among other thing the town drum. It was in this room we settled down for a glass divination experiment. The idea behind divination is that by touching a glass lightly with your fingertips and asking a series of questions, a spirit can communicate by moving it across a flat surface, such as a board or table. The lights were turned out, and by the glow of a torch, questions were asked while the rapt gathering waited in silent anticipation. The glass stayed still for what seemed an age, despite repeated questions it remained stationary, until it began to slowly move, rotating slightly before stopping. As we concentrated in the hope of capturing further movement a deep voice mumbled something in my left ear. Somewhat perturbed, and in the near dark, I called out to the only other male in the group asking if he had said something to me, and his quaking and high pitched reply coming from an entirely different part of the room convinced me he had not. After the initial 'mumblings' and nervous exchanges that preceded this event quietened down the group continued to ask for the glass to be moved, but despite willing with all our might, nothing else happened. Feeling slightly disheartened and somewhat stiff from sitting on the cold flagstones we repaired to base camp and had coffee, before proceeding to the condemned cell and our next vigil. In this cell it was decided to sit quietly for a while to see if any activity would occur and the lights were put out. In the darkness there was virtual silence apart from the sound of breathing and the odd shuffle as people tried to get comfortable on the stone floor. After a while some members of the group began to comment on their difficulty in getting breath while others complained of a tightening round their necks. The vigil was temporarily halted as one participant, after feeling too 'ill' to continue decided to leave the room. At this point and unnoticed till then, we became aware of a cold spot in the corner of the room where the absentee had previously been sitting. We stood in a circle before the spot and stretching out our hands could feel a tangible temperature change. In the near darkness I aimed my camera at the corner of the room and took three shots in quick succession. Two were normal whilst the third showed a strange orange light at floor level which came from no identifiable source. Perplexed as to its source and finding no further activity, the vigil continued until we were called back downstairs. Dawn came and as the groups met to swap experiences it became apparent that much of the activity was centred round the same areas. Some names had been picked up and a number of light anomalies captured on film including one seen with the naked eye. It had been an interesting experience though given the noises I had heard on previous visits perhaps I had expected too much of the evening. The event, though enjoyable, left me in no doubt as to the nature of spirit which has free will and cannot be cajoled into 'performing' unless it wishes to. I have found that the old adage of being in the right place at the right time is true and believe that the best evidence is often gathered in a state of peace which is hard to achieve with large crowds of people and so for the moment I decided to leave the Tolbooth.

Despite further visits to the Tolbooth all has been, though to back up my belief that the building is prone to sporadic activity, I was told the following. In 2005 Mrs. Wood had been visiting the museum with her husband and her friend's son aged around eight. Mrs. Wood recounts: "I went up the stair and could hear a wifie greeting (a mannequin situated on the top floor). I was looking at the board (information panel) on the first floor and as I turned to speak to my husband I saw a little man about 4ft. high, wearing a brown striped suit and a brown hat from the 1920s, a Trilby hat." She went on to say: "He nodded his head at me but didn't speak. I ran out, jumped six steps at a time and ran onto Union Street where the man at the door shouted after me if I was okay. I went back and told him what I saw and he said I wasn't the first person to see him. He offered me a drink of water as I was sweating so much." As it transpired neither her husband nor the child saw anything as they were looking the other way and were perplexed as to why she had made a rapid exit, assuming she had felt unwell. Mrs. Wood concluded by saying: "She has never gone back there." She remains adamant as to what she saw. I must admit, I was heartened to hear this account as I had automatically assumed that if there was any spirit activity in the building it would have to be related to its time as a prison rather than much later. The description of the figure in 1920s/30s clothing could certainly tie in with a council employee of the period whose duties may have included that of building management, as in the 1900s, those rooms became a wine store and records store for the council. Mrs. Wood's vivid description also made mention of his short stature. Was he really that short in stature or perhaps as seen in other cases, the level of the floors had been altered from when he was alive leaving a portion of the leg hidden. This is certainly an argument that is not without substance as it is known that most of the floors in the Tolbooth have been upgraded in recent years with flagstones replacing the original brick.

And so, on that note I leave the Tolbooth for the time being. Though I remain convinced that there is activity at the Tolbooth, I would suggest that perhaps it not as prevalent as one might suspect given its dark past. Whoever has been sensed there, and they have been, is more than likely in visitation due in no small part to the sporadic nature of their appearances. After all, with its dark past, and given the choice would you want to live there permanently?

Hazelhead Academy

One of the most baffling and unusual series of events is connected to this modern building. Situated on the outskirts of the city, this building is allegedly home to a spirit, which appears to enjoy participating in youth theatre. I first came upon the story when I was searching for evidence of the elusive Captain Beaton. I had made a tentative enquiry to the Gordon Highlanders Museum, asking if they had anything in their archive relating to his army records. During my visit I got chatting to one of the volunteers / researchers at the museum. The volunteer as it transpired was a teacher from Hazelhead Academy and he proceeded to tell me about his colleague in the drama department who believed there is a spirit or spirits haunting the stage area. He suggested I give him a phone if I was interested in finding out more, and I did not need to be asked twice. From the initial call, I was invited to conduct an interview with the head of the department and was offered the opportunity to look round the active area.

The academy though relatively new, being built in the late 1960s, was on land that had been formerly part of the forest of Stocket. The story goes that Robert the Bruce gifted it to the people of Aberdeen for their support in the war against the English. In reality Aberdeen was granted custodianship at a price. The yearly feu or payment at that time, amounted to £ 213 6s 8d sterling, which was a considerable amount of money in1319. The land remained thus until 1553, before being feud out to others, and used for arable farming. It changed hands on a number of occasions. In 1775 a mansion was built for the Rose family in what is now Hazelhead Park. A beautiful building, it stood until 1959 when the council unwisely decided to demolish it, replacing it with the current building. The current café, though invoking a sense of nostalgia for many Aberdonians, is not the most aesthetically pleasing of buildings, and one cannot help but wonder, how the park would have been enhanced by the survival of the mansion. The Donaldson Rose family were ship owners who, like many other estate owners, found themselves selling off pockets of land as times changed and belts tightened. A large amount of land was sold to create Hazelhead golf course, and the trend continued in 1920 when the council bought back much of the rest for £40,000, with the aim of building the much loved Hazelhead Park. The market garden and nurseries occupying the site of the current school also went and the land lay unused. In the late 1960s with the number of school age children growing it was decided to build a new school. Taking children from other established seats of learning it offered contemporary education in a modern setting. As mentioned, unlike other 'haunted locations' this is a relatively new building and the land around it does not appear to have been host to any notable past tragedies. There was however a rumour that the school was built on a pre- Victorian graveyard, but this has been proven to be unfounded as no records I can find, suggest it ever existed. I also lived for a while in the area, and though too young to remember, my dad mentioned that before the school was built there was only farm land, which unfortunately gives no indication as to who has been seen in the building.

Chris, head of the drama department is rightly proud of being involved with the school's youth theatre, Channel Five, citing it as the longest running in the city, since its formation in the 1980s. It has had many successes, though it also appears to have become something of a magnet for the unwanted attention of a spirit, which is predominately seen during production times. According to reports, it seems keen to let itself be known when there are other children about, as during performance times, its activities step up a gear, and a pervading feeling of gloom becomes apparent. Staff, busy with rehearsals, began to be aware of a feeling of depression within the vicinity of the stage, prop and staff room, the atmosphere being described as charged and still, with sound appearing muffled like the calm before the storm. Small incidents began to occur, unexplained cold spots appeared, unusual feelings were sensed and sudden drafts became prevalent.

It was enough to get staff talking and people began to feel nervous in the area, especially when it was quiet. Noise phenomena continued to occur, with loud knocks being heard on the thin plasterboard walls partitioning the rooms, and when staff investigated no cause could be found. Things took a dramatic turn, when during a coffee break, a number of witnesses saw a spoon 'jump' out of an empty cup, enough to prompt one teacher to start taking her break in another part of the building. Also, as in many theatres, the curtains are weighted with chains to stop movement during a performance, and these would rattle loudly of their own accord, being normally too heavy to do so unless assisted.

I arrived with a colleague on a bright May afternoon, full of anticipation after getting a selection of highlights over the phone. After the introductions, I was given a tour of the prop area, which though small and cramped, was full of interesting objects relating to past productions. We were told the prop and scenery areas were the most active, and were frequently plagued by unusual occurrences. As if on cue, I was instantly aware of someone with us. My colleague also became aware of this and remarked how cold and shivery he felt. As Chris continued to show us around, the feeling remained, as if someone was close by listening in, until we walked onto the stage area when it suddenly went. The scenery room, we were told, is notorious for engendering a feeling of being watched, which has been reported by both staff and pupils alike. It appeared that pupils had also complained of being 'touched' by something during rehearsal times. It was mentioned, that during the production of 'The Little Shop of Horrors' a female pupil was changing costume in the privacy booth, when a 'small, freezing cold child's hand came over her shoulder, and touched her'. She described the hand as appearing to be 'stretching'. This had occurred, as she had been putting on a 'beehive wig' at the mirror, and could clearly see the hand reflected in the mirror, though surprisingly, she did not feel overly frightened by the incident. Things, we were told, quietened down again apart from the odd feelings and unexplained noises until when during a production of 'The Crucible' what was

119

described, as the image of 'the face of a screaming woman' appeared amongst the scumbled paint of the backdrop. The teacher, on having his attention drawn to this by a pupil, noticed that in the vicinity of the 'face' the air was icy cold, so much so that he stated: "My throat was sore like being outside on a raw winter's day." He immediately went and got a colleague, who also witnessed the phenomena. The painted image could well have been created accidentally through the scumbling of the paint, they concurred, but it could not explain the freezing temperature. The temperature eventually returned to what was normal for the area.

During this time staff made every effort to try and keep things going as 'normal' by trying to rationalise things for the sake of the pupils, and treating it lightly, though it was common knowledge that the area was rumoured to be haunted. In 2005 perhaps the most baffling event occurred during the production of 'Blood Brothers' when an analogue camera (CCTV for the stage) showed a small boy on stage leaning against a pillar, arms folded, watching the rehearsals. As Chris explained, this had been picked up on the monitor and witnessed by eight different people, including the stage manager. One staff member, John, (who was described as ex- army and not prone to flights of fancy) was also witness to this. No one could offer a reasonable explanation for what was happening. The boy in question, was described as 'wearing a 1960s Paisley top and shorts, and appeared completely solid, though he did not move'. The strangest aspect of it all however, was he could only be seen through the monitor, as when staff looked directly at the stage he was invisible to the naked eye. No one could rationally explain these events and it was stated as being 'disturbing' for the witnesses. I admit that I was feeling uneasy, as I had the feeling that whoever was responsible, liked playing tricks on people. Even without malice it was still behaviour likely to cause alarm.

Chris put forward a number of theories as to why he thought these events were occurring. One was that, it was rumoured, the school had been built on the site of an ancient graveyard, though even if it had existed, which is unlikely, it did not explain why the boy was wearing what could be described as contemporary clothing. The other theory offered was that a former janitor claimed a workman was killed during the construction of the school and was perhaps still around. In defence of this theory, it has been recorded on numerous occasions that the spirits of those killed in tragic circumstances may be responsible for what is tantamount to poltergeist activities, as a means of communicating their frustration. However, I personally felt, it was more likely to be the spirit of someone who had lived locally, and being involved with the school is drawn back at times wishing to interact with other children. This is only a theory, and I could be missing the mark by a mile, but as there is no definite evidence as to the spirit's identity we can only surmise. I was impressed by the quality of the information given, and of the detail involved, and felt everyone was very genuine about what they saw. I decided to return at a later date to see if there had been any other activity and thanked everyone involved in what was an interesting visit.

In early 2007, I felt the time was right to pay another visit. I was rewarded by meeting two new staff members, who, by their own admission, were sceptical at first, though witnessed a number of incidents during 'activities week', which had changed their point of view. Morag, who was very sceptical about the stories at first, was sitting in the staff room when she heard a noise, and went out to the stage area to investigate. She noticed that a large piece of paper with hand written notes on it had fallen from the wall, and was lying, where she described, 'it shouldn't be'. She went over to retrieve it, and was greeted by the sight of one of the corners flapping continually, though there was no apparent draft. A sceptic, could argue, that this could have been explained, but what happened next was disconcerting to say the least.

If anyone needed convincing that the area was haunted, then the following erased any doubts. After a busy day the staff were catching up and the conversation turned to the unusual events that had been taking place. Chris suggested that they go into the prop room, turn off the lights, and for 'a laugh' ask for some evidence from the spirit. They stood in the room, which I might add lets in very little light, while Chris jokingly called out for any spirit to let themselves be known. Nothing happened. They stood for a number of minutes and were about to leave, when to everyone's surprise, three bright blue balls of light shot past the prop room shelving in quick succession, disappearing through the outer wall. They were described to me as having 'light tails and leaving a residue'. Chris went on to say, that the residue illuminated an old telephone on a table below, leaving it 'glowing for about two seconds'. They panicked, it was suddenly not funny anymore, and the lights were put on before they left promptly. This however was not the end of it, as Chris discovered. When he arrived the next day he found that the tools, which hang on the far wall had been interfered with. The four saws, which normally hang on hooks, had been moved and placed blade down into a narrow slot. As Chris approached the work area, gingerly, and reached out to touch the saws, they promptly fell, with the resulting crash causing him to jump. He stated that 'there was no way they could have fallen on their own and landed neatly into the slot'. He, along with other staff are still at a loss as to who is causing the activity and what circumstances are keeping them attached to the area. It remains a mystery. The general consensus among staff is that whoever is causing this, and it may possibly be down to more than one spirit, is definitely not around all the time, as on most days there is no discernible activity. It would appear that the energy generated during production time is a huge factor in attracting the spirit, and though mischievous, appears to want to draw attention to itself and participate. There is no outcome to this story, no definite facts, as to who it might be, but there is a huge amount of anecdotal evidence from a diverse group of professionals to give credence to these events. I have no reason to doubt these stories. Firstly, I am no conspiracy theorist and don't believe that people get together in groups to make these tales up, and it's certainly not been told for money or publicity. I was also very aware of someone's energy when I first visited the drama department, as was my colleague, a fact I am still convinced of, and for me that is evidence enough. The activity continues to this day with recent reports of voices being heard by a teacher as he painted a set. On turning round to see who had entered the room, he found there was no one there.

When I was first heard of the activity in the school there were a number of theories going around as to its cause, the school being built on the sight of a graveyard was one. This proved unfounded but it was pointed out to me recently that there is an old graveyard, in the vicinity of Maidencraig nature reserve, situated not to far from the school. The area was historically known as Gilla Hill and nearby was a graveyard, used allegedly by the university for the disposal of bodies used by anatomists in the early 1800s. The practice was allegedly discontinued in the 1830s. When in the library I discovered a photograph of an ancient looking mound surrounded by trees, in a book on the freedom lands of Aberdeen. The caption read 'Gilla Hill and cemetery from Gallow Hill'. There is apparently a debate over whether there was a Gallows Hill, but what is known, is that the place of judgement was at Fairley Den where there was a Justice Cairn less than half a mile from Gilla Hill. There are many crossroads running off the hill, and gallows were historically often at crossroads. It probably does not have any connection to the haunting but at least the rumour of a graveyard nearby has some truth to it. On a final note, I met someone in a work related capacity recently. We got chatting about the projects we were involved with and I casually mentioned my research at Hazelhead. She mentioned that, she had grown up in the area around the time of the school being opened, and remembered that someone she knew, a young boy, was killed in a farm accident near to the school.

Castlehill Barracks

This story happened just after World War Two and though the building in question has long since vanished, I felt it was so intriguing, that I had to include it. The story was related to me, by that fine singer, musician and storyteller Stanley Robertson, who has kindly allowed me to use it in this book. It was related to him by his school friend's mother, and took place in the Castlehill barracks. The barracks were built in 1794 for the Gordon Highlanders, and used by the regiment until 1935 when they were moved to their new headquarters at the Bridge of Don. After the war and prior to its demolition, it was used as a temporary measure to alleviate a housing shortage, offering cheap but inadequate housing, eventually being classed as slum dwellings.

By 1965, the site was cleared for redevelopment as multi story housing, and with the construction of Virginia Court and Marischal Court, the area was changed forever. The building itself was a sprawling Georgian construction, being a prominent feature of the Castlegate until the arrival of the Salvation Army 'citadel' in 1896, which in its grandeur promptly overshadowed its more elderly neighbours. The site unfortunately, is unrecognisable today. However it is worth noting that up until the 1960s and 1970s much of the area still retained many fine buildings, sadly now demolished with little regard for their historic value. These included the old Sick Children's Hospital, the Virginia Buildings and other fine town houses, which were built into the hill leading to what is now Virginia Court. The area itself has a grim history, the self explanatory 'heading hill', Commerce Street, scene of witch burnings and the nearby 'Hangman's Brae', all sit in close proximity giving the area, according to some, an unpleasant 'vibe' at times. As mentioned, after the First and particularly the Second World War, there was a huge demand for housing and expanding families left the council struggling to cope with the population's growth. It was a time of 'make do' with many people forced to take inappropriate lodgings out of necessity. This was certainly the case with the mum in question, who after marrying young was left with two young children, and was forced to take lodgings in the run down former barracks.

It was just after the end of the war and things were tight for most people. Her husband, on returning from the war became a 'hawker' and spent more and more time away from home, leaving his young wife to fend for herself and look for accommodation. She was described in those days as being 'the spitting image of Hedi Lamar' and an acquaintance of the family who worked as a factor, and a key holder for the Castlehill Barracks, was 'quite taken with her'. This, no doubt was instrumental in him to trying to find her accommodation, and fairly soon she was offered a place. It was described as being 'across the big square of the barracks, past the married quarters, then across the wee brig over Commerce Street to the old military hospital'. She was offered a basement room in the barracks for a knockdown price of literally pence, and promptly took it. Stanley remembers the room being down three flights of stairs in the 'sunks' of the building, where there was no working stair light. At the bottom of the stairs lay a solitary door and behind it a huge long room with no windows. The room was painted a 'nondescript greenish murky colour', and even with the antiquated gas lights on it provided very little illumination, and the fact there was no natural light added to the grim surroundings, 'everything was made of stone and extremely dark'. Not long after they moved in the youngest child, Shirley fell ill. Her fever was bad enough to cause her mother serious concern, and she went round the neighbours in the upper floors to ask if they had any medicine she could borrow, but they had none. She had no money and there were certainly no chemists around which opened at night. One neighbour suggested that 'she go by the nearby district nurses headquarters, Ingleborough House, and ask for assistance'. The building in question was a centre for both district nurses and Queen Anne nurses. Taking the neighbour's advice, she approached the nursing station and spoke to the nurse at reception, asking if there was anyone willing to make a house call. As the nurse was the only one on duty she was unable to leave the building, but said that if anyone came back she would ask them to drop by. She returned home and waited anxiously by her daughter's bed. The fever remained constant, and she was beside herself with worry. She had all but given up hope of anyone assisting when she heard a noise outside the door, and rushing to open it, found a nurse standing in the gloom. The nurse was ushered in, taken to the patient, and immediately sat by her bed. She remained virtually silent but appeared to be tending the young patient and signaled that the mother should sit down and rest. After some hours the nurse rose and left. The grateful mother, noticing that Shirley was resting easier, spent the remainder of the night dozing by her bed. By the morning her daughter's condition had improved so much that she felt able to leave her for a short while. She went down to the nurses' home to pass on her thanks only to be met with a blank stare. They had not sent anyone down, being busy all night with more urgent cases. Perplexed she described the nurse and to her surprise was told that there was no nurse of that description and in fact the uniform described was that of a nurse from the First World War. A short time later a startling piece of information came to light, their home at Castlehill Barracks, the room with no windows and ghastly green walls, was used as a mortuary during that period.

This story intrigued me and I did a cursory sweep of the Post Office Directories of the time as a matter of course. Interestingly the area described in the story contained not only the barracks and the associated military hospital but more importantly the district nurses headquarters which sat on top of the old heading hill. As the building is unfortunately long gone the situation does not allow an investigation or visit to take place. Given the circumstances of the story it would appear that the spirit in question still felt the need to continue to care for the ill even after her physical death. Historically there have been many tales associated with nurses and doctors appearing in times of crisis to comfort the ill or dying. As an aside my sister in law, who works for a hospital trust in Milton Keynes, has told me stories on numerous occasions relating to colleagues who have passed on and yet continue to visit unwitting patients, offering solace. In fact hospitals are so inextricably linked to spirit activity that one almost becomes blasé when hearing of such tales. Stanley went on to say that the mother is still alive today and remembers the incident 'vividly'.

Provost Skenes House

This is one of only a few 16th century buildings left in the city and would have suffered the same fate as the others has it not been for the intervention of the Queen Mother, who having voiced her disapproval at council plans to demolish it during the redevelopment of the Guestrow area, stayed its destruction. It was saved, renovated, and is now run by the City Council as a museum. With a colourful past, from family home to common lodging house the building has borne witness to many events over the centuries and in my opinion and that of many staff and visitors is haunted and very active with full figure manifestations being witnessed. To give a little background to the buildings history the house was first mentioned in the sasine register of 1545 with the owner noted as Alexander Knollis a member of a wealthy land owning family. From 1585-1622 the house was then owned by a succession of wealthy people including a Laird and a Bishop, until latterly owned by a bankrupt. Initially a three story rectangular tower, it was subsequently added too by the Knollis family and then by Baillie Mathew Lumsden who owned the building from 1622 till around 1641. As an aside, during this turbulent period he fought and died for the Covenanter cause at the Battle of Justice Mills and like many other victims of the battle his burial place is now unknown. Wealthy merchant and Provost, Sir George Skene created further changes during his subsequent ownership by changing the window elevations, flattening the roof, building the east staircase and turrets and creating the beautiful plaster ceilings that remain to this day. The house continued to be occupied by Skene's family relatives until 1732. During the ensuing years the infamous Duke of Cumberland occupied the house on his way to defeat the Jacobites at Culloden, much to the chagrin of many locals. It was this event that was instrumental in it being known as Cumberland House though around this time it was divided into east and west houses and remained this way for a hundred years when again it became one dwelling house.

The next owner of note was Walter Duthie owner from 1844 to 1870, a writer to the signet of Edinburgh it was during his ownership that the building became a 'House of Refuge'. Philanthropist Miss Elizabeth Duthie who gifted the Duthie Park to the city then owned the property and in 1879 leased it out as the renamed Victoria Lodging House. Despite changing names the house remained as a lodging-house until its closure in 1951. During this period patrons could gain entry with a token for what must have been an uncomfortable night's sleep as their bed consisted of nothing more than the support of a rope hung across the, as then, undiscovered painted gallery. Apart from being terribly uncomfortable I have been told that the old practice of letting down the rope in the morning none to gently was still used. From the few photographs of the interior that exist it must have been a Spartan existence. The whitewashed walls did little to alleviate the grim surroundings, with men crouched over feeble fires to keep warm, giving a Dickensian feel to the rooms. Though suggesting squalor, the image presented was fairly typical of common lodging houses of the time of which there were a number in the city. In the 1930s the council came to the decision to demolish much of the surrounding streets which had fallen from the once fashionable to one of the most deprived slum areas in the city. The building now stood alone. It was during the 1951 refurbishment of the Long Gallery in the Lumsden west wing that a series of tempera-painted panels were uncovered depicting the Life of Christ. They are considered among the finest of the remaining examples in Scotland and were lucky to survive being hidden for many years. Interestingly during the course of my research I have met a number of people who have had connections to the house, one in particular remembers playing outside the building in the 1930s when the area was still a rabbit warren of old houses and lanes. He described it as a 'great place to play as a kid' and how they had great adventures there despite the areas down at heel image. The house is situated in what was the residential part of Guest Row which is first mentioned in a charter from 1439 referring to 'Vicus Lemurum' which is Latin for the ironically named 'street of spectres'. This name was apparently given due to its proximity to St. Nicholas Kirkyard and possibly in a belief that it was haunted.

In the late 1960s the council took the decision, in my opinion an unforgivable one, to knock down most of the remaining buildings of character in the immediate area and construct a series of unappealing monoliths in their place. This race to modernise, a trend not only confined to Aberdeen, resulted in one of the city's most historic properties being hemmed in by its overbearing neighbours, essentially making it invisible from the main thoroughfare. With Broad Street's development practically rendering the building invisible it remains undiscovered to this day by many. I first became aware of the house when as a tutor I used the building for location drawing. During the aforementioned drawing classes I became acquainted with the staff and in time the conversation inevitably turned to the supernatural. Feeling comfortable enough in their company to mention that I had sensed a presence on a number of occasions, I was surprised to be told I was not alone in sensing this and so began probably one of the most interesting researches I have ever undertaken. There is no record of any incidents being reported during its time as a lodging house with the earliest reports I could find dating from more recent times when a number of inexplicable events came to light. During one of our Friday morning conversations staff member Raymond mentioned that the first incidents he was aware of began as far back as the mid 1980s and so began a prolonged period of research where I was lucky enough to interview many people connected to the building. The rooms of the house are atmospheric and are furnished with items reflecting changes in style since the building was first inhabited including rooms from both the 17th century and Regency period. It also includes temporary exhibition rooms on the top floor of the building. It has been noted that locking up at night when the building is visitor free is not the most popular of tasks especially as some of the rooms have a peculiar atmosphere and staff delegated this duty are never keen to linger.

The incidents about to be related have occurred throughout the house though some rooms are more notorious than others for distilling a sense of foreboding among staff.

The west wing of the house contains a number of fine plaster ceilings and reflects the oldest period of the house, with the 17th century parlour and bedroom being particularly prone to activity. The following incident was related to me by a member of staff, who on hearing raised voices in the west wing went to investigate. As it transpired the commotion was caused by two visitors, a mother and daughter, who was convinced her mother had shoved her out the way at the doorway of the bedroom causing her to stumble and was vocalising her grievance. The mother on the other hand was adamant she had been looking at the 17th century parlour and as she had been facing the other way was in no way responsible for 'barging past her'. The situation was diffused and they left soon after leaving staff to ponder over the incident. As to the pusher, this remains a mystery, though incidents of visitors being jostled have been noted on a number of occasions since. The turret leading up from the aforementioned rooms has also been prone to activity as demonstrated one evening when Stevie, a former employee was descending the staircase. He became aware of footsteps behind him and thinking a visitor was still inside at locking up time went back up to investigate. Finding no one there he descended once more only to have the noise of footsteps, now directly behind, follow him downstairs. He ran for it, 'switched the alarm on and fled'. Continuing in the west wing one visitor recently complained to staff of being unable to enter the painted gallery due to the room 'being full of people'. It transpired she had tried to open the door and feeling someone pushing against it could only open it marginally. What she saw inside was described as a crowd and being slightly annoyed at not gaining access mentioned this to staff asking if there was an event on. The staff assured the visitor that being first thing in the morning she was the first visitor but on her insistence went to look and on investigation found the room empty.

One particular incident stands out and in no way can be contributed to imagination. The incident again occurred in the 17th century parlour but this time at the end of the day. The staff member in question recalled that as she prepared to lock up she became aware of someone entering the room. She swung round and witnessed 'the ghost of a woman, dressed in old fashioned clothes with dark hair' coming into the room. The figure stopped and they faced each other, frozen to the spot she watched the figure disappear. She described to me that it appeared: "As solid as I am," and went on to say: "I got the impression she saw me as well." This occurrence was enough to confirm her suspicions. She stated: "I was very shocked and not quite sure if I really saw her, it happened so quickly, but I do know what I saw was real after a lot of arguing with myself." She concluded by saying: "There has been a lot of people living at Provost Skene's House so I think there are a few different presence's." The spirit energies in the house though strong at times could not be described as malevolent, though there is a sense of unhappiness some areas. During my many visits I got the impression that most of the activity is from a female who if not permanently there is certainly a frequent visitor. She is proud of her house and happy that people enjoy visiting it though appears to have her own agenda. I believe her to be active rather than residual mainly due to the fact she is not following any pattern of behaviour, she has been seen in many parts of the house and appears to have interacted with staff and visitors on a number of occasions. The overall feeling is that she had position and was probably an owner at some point, one staff member believes her to be Elisabeth Aberdour wife of Mathew Lumsden as she appeared to her wearing clothes from that era. The staircase leading down from the 17th century parlour is shut to the public but leads down to the old kitchen and it was here that another full figure manifestation was witnessed by staff from the café. Working in the kitchen one morning they noticed someone out of the corner of their eye outside the door and immediately assumed that someone had gained entry to the old kitchen .As the building was still shut they decided to confront the person to let her know it was not yet open to the public. Only in retrospect did they wonder why they never questioned the fact she was 'dressed up' wearing an 'old dress and crinoline bonnet' being more concerned that someone had 'broken in' They received quite a shock as when approached the figure, she suddenly disappeared.

As you can imagine these occurrences were more than intriguing and I continued to visit regularly chatting to staff waiting for the magic words 'something happened last week' when I would haul out my pen and notepad scribbling furiously. I also began to enjoy the frequent encounters I would have with spirit, sensing a benign presence. I got the impression that because I loved the house so much my presence was at the least tolerated. Some time later I was in the rooms at the top of the house, where I had gone along to see a display of Seaton pottery. As this is an area where normally there is little activity I was surprised to see in my minds eye a small man dressed in black with a very long grey beard. He walked towards me, bent over, and appeared to be coughing though he did not notice me. It only lasted seconds but so clear was the impression that I still remember it vividly. I continued down the staircase and was aware of his presence and the accompanying chill until I reached the next floor down when he went out of the atmosphere. It was these impressions that lead me to conclude that the house was home to different spirit people from different eras and certainly activity has occurred in all parts of the building as is demonstrated by the following account. The house attracts visitors of all ages and on one occasion two girls in their late teens were accompanying their younger sister who staff believed to be around six years of age. They were asked when leaving if they had enjoyed their visit, which they had apart from the fact the young girl had complained of 'being followed by a man from room to room'. The elder siblings kept looking round and could see no one despite the youngsters continuing protestations. The young girl claimed that he was 'always there' and though not afraid felt perplexed as to why he was following her. The older girls laughed it off saying to the museum assistant that it was her imagination getting the better of her. The staff member in question made light of the situation but was well aware that there was no one else upstairs at that time and certainly no male staff members on duty that day.

Generally the most frequent type of activity is aural as demonstrated by the following incident which occurred in September 2006. Eileen and her colleague were on duty at the time and explained: "We were in our workroom preparing to open up when we both heard heavy footsteps echoing up the main staircase to the house. We both looked at each other and initially thought the door had been left open and someone had come in early not realising we were still closed. We went to check the door and it was still locked, we then went up stairs to double check and of course as we suspected the building was empty. This happens a lot." She went on to say that what she finds most annoying is seeing movement out of the corner of her eye and when looking round gets the distinct impression of someone moving out of view, this has become such a regular occurrence that she has more than once said out loud 'for God's sake, show yourself!' The most recent activity of this nature occurred in November 2006 when Sandy, who works at the house, was on the top floor and heard someone walking around in the adjoining room. As the two rooms were connected by an open door, he went through to see who was there only to discover the room empty and when going downstairs found the front door was still locked. He explained: "The floor is wooden and very noisy when walked on." And therefore he could find no rational explanation as to what caused the noise as his colleague had remained at the front door. He readily admits that he is a sceptic but has found the many experiences he has witnessed baffling and when I uttered the word 'cool' when hearing of the footsteps he remarked: "Well it wasn't cool for me." As mentioned the house has two distinct wings and not to be out done the east wing has had its fair share of activity as can be seen with the following. The east wing is home to the Regency rooms which have a small painted gallery connecting them. At night staff are required to lock the connecting doors and many feel this area to be particularly claustrophobic. The first incident of note occurred some years ago in the early 1990s when an attendant opening the aforementioned doors for an evening function became aware of someone standing directly behind him. He stood stock still, feeling his scalp crawl before bolting from the room. His colleague was shocked to see him appear, looking 'like a bucket of water had been thrown over him' and being 'completely soaked in sweat'. Obviously distressed he took some time to regain his composure. Others have mentioned that they don't have a good feeling in this area including a number of children—my daughter included—who seem to be more sensitive to the atmosphere of the Regency rooms. In another incident, which happened more recently, an assistant found a member of the public standing outside the rooms looking bewildered and unable to go in. When asked if she was feeling alright she replied that she was 'aware that some people were in there, discussing something important and felt it was not right to disturb them'. The staff member being perplexed did not push the matter but it is known that a number of visitors have been 'stopped' from entering certain rooms and complained of having 'barriers' put up against them. It is interesting to note that these feelings have also been felt by museum assistants as demonstrated when a member of staff was making her way down the east wing turret when opening up. The attendant in question was making her way down the turret and was directly in front of the heavy wooden door when she became aware of raised voices behind the door. The voices lowered and continued to mutter and she was convinced that she was hearing 'an argument'. After being frozen to the spot for some seconds she decided to confront who ever it was and opened it quickly stepping through to be met with silence. Again no explanation can be found, though voices especially whispering have been heard on numerous occasions in this area. Perhaps the most interesting evidence came through the experience of a visitor who was in the house before Christmas 2006. She was the only member of the public upstairs at the time and apart from Sandy and one other on duty, the building was empty. Sandy witnessed the aftermath of her experience and recounts: "We were in the office when a middle aged lady came down the stairs, she appeared to be flustered and explained that she had been in the Regency room and had continued into the small painted gallery when she was confronted by the sight of a woman sitting on the chaise long. The visitor got quite a shock and turned and ran before she could see what the figure did although she saw it was wearing a long dark dress and lace cap. I immediately went up the stairs to find the seat empty and no sign of the woman." After calming down the visitor left, what interested me most about the figure described was that it was different to that of the lady seen in the 17th century parlour and lends credence to the notion that there are a number of different spirits present. Though not able to visit as regularly as I would like I still catch up with staff and was recently informed that in March 2007 an electrician was working in the Regency room. As he worked he was overcome by a feeling of immense sadness and 'he felt the hair on his neck rise' as if someone was directly behind him watching. He was so perturbed by the incident he mentioned it to staff who subsequently found that he had never been in the building before and knew nothing of its history.

Personally I am in no doubt as to the authenticity of these experiences and given the sheer volume of activity and the fact these occurrences have been ongoing for years it is very surprising that these have never been recorded before. There is a variety of feelings associated with certain rooms especially a sense of sadness which has been noted on occasion though given the unhappy lives of former residents a residue is likely to remain. On a final note I have found investigating Provost Skene's House an enriching experience though I would suggest that anyone wishing to investigate a location should treat spirit and their 'property' with the same respect as you would when visiting someone on the physical plane. In my opinion, television programmes like 'Most Haunted' perhaps inadvertently, do a great disservice to furthering an understanding of the motivations of a spirit when their sole objective appears to be one of antagonising. Showing disrespect and displaying arrogance by aggressively challenging serves no purpose other than to titillate the viewer and is without a doubt going to be detrimental to any investigation and should be avoided. I personally would ask nicely and hopefully receive a positive response though ultimately it is down to the spirit person in question and whether they want to participate. On a personal note I intend to continue to visit this fascinating house and would recommend you do the same whether your interests lie with the paranormal or not.

The Ministry and the Pallas

Though there has not historically been any documented activity attached to this building, I thought the story, being contemporary, warranted inclusion. The Ministry formerly The Ministry of Sin was one of Aberdeen's most established clubs and a mainstay for many since the 1980s. Currently under refurbishment, it was during the alterations of the interior, and the removal of a wall, that a number of unexplained incidents occurred resulting in one worker leaving the site and refusing to return. The building was present in town maps of the mid 1800s when it was situated in what was known as New Dee Street. Originally used as a congregational church, it became redundant until 1882 when the Free Gaelic Church moved in from their former Gaelic Lane premises, renaming it St. Columba Free Church. In 1900, following a split, the main body of the congregation followed their minister into the United Free Church, while the rest remained, being allocated the Dee Street premises permanently in 1907. This situation lasted until 1977 when they too moved, leaving the building vacant, which was subsequently turned into a nightclub.

As far as I am aware nothing unusual happened during this period, and there are no recorded incidents to suggest otherwise. In 2006 the papers ran an article reporting that during the current alterations ghostly faces were allegedly captured on camera in front of the aforementioned wall. The story was brought to my attention by a friend, who having seen the article in the paper thought I would be interested. I contacted the current owner Mike and was given permission to take some photographs of the interior and speak to the contractors, though he did say that the activity seemed to have died down. I went round to see the building some days later and had the opportunity to meet with some of those involved. Patrick, who had previously been quoted in the papers about the incidents took me upstairs to a vast open plan room and told me that one day the lights had started to swing of their own accord even though there was no draft. One of the workers had stated at the time that 'that if the lights went out, then he was off.' Someone was obviously very obliging as that is exactly what happened causing panic among the contractors and a refusal by some to work on their own.

Another interesting event, which occurred on the same floor, was the sound of footsteps running when there has been no one around and voices heard in conversation, which would stop abruptly. The sound of footsteps apparently continued over a period of time and was the most repetitive of the activities reported. Given the nature of the location, basically a building site, there would obviously have been a lot of noise and movement in the area and some of the more sceptical members of the team cited nerves and imagination as causing concern rather than anything supernatural.

While on the top floor I was able to view the ceiling beams and the original carvings that line the walls, this being one of the few areas, apart from the main structure, where original architecture can be seen. It was while I was there I noticed the exposed granite wall at the front of the building and took some shots for posterity. I was interested to notice, that despite the huge amount of dust orbs present on the images, there was one unusually bright orb, for want of a better term, which appeared to be moving. I then went down to the basement and spoke to two electricians, one local and one from Hull, who verified that the lighting had been acting up since they started the contract, even though they could find no reason why it should. During the conversation, and as if on cue, the bulb next to where I stood went out, we laughed, albeit nervously, as there was a slight tension in the air. We stood chatting about events and they mentioned that the images of children's faces had been captured on a camera phone by the acting site manager Simon. They were alleged to have appeared against the partly demolished wall. It was at this point, I was suddenly aware of a cold chill in the air. I thought it was best not to mention this, as both the electricians were appeared a bit jumpy. It felt like someone was listening in to

139

our conversation, and to add to the mood, the light next to me sprang into life, going on again, while its companion next door decided, it was its turn to go out. "See, see," they chorused. They were both unsure as to why the lights were being affected, and I mentioned that if it was a spirit, then one of the ways they can let themselves be known, is by tampering with electrical appliances and lighting. One stated that he did believe the activity to be of supernatural origin, mentioning that he heard there was supposed to be a grave yard at the back of the building many years ago.

The conversation continued, and he proceeded to tell me that some years ago, a frightening occurrence had left a friend of his in a state of alarm, causing him to leave the job he was on. The man in question, also an electrician, had been working on the stairs of what was originally known as the New Pallas Theatre on Bridge Place. As he worked, his concentration was broken, and he became aware of an approaching noise. He pinned himself against the wall as the sound of muffled but panicked voices increased in volume. A rush of air, as if a large number of people were moving quickly, rushed past him at speed leaving him frozen to the spot. He was so shaken by the incident and being unable to offer any rational explanation, left quickly without finishing the job. I decided to leave, promising to return, and some days later, while looking through a book on historic Aberdeen, I came across an interesting story. On the 30th of September 1896 the theatre, then known as the People's Palace was the scene of a terrible fire in which seven people perished. It transpired that during a performance, part of the stage set had brushed against a gas jet and almost instantly a fire had started in the 'fly' area. Despite the best efforts of staff it could not be contained and the fire took hold quickly. Before half the audience had the opportunity to leave, the flames had rushed along the wooden structures ceiling and reached one of the exits. Reports at the time stated, that crowds were forced to flee in panic and many were injured in the ensuing crush. This terrible fire was one of many to hit British Theatres at that time, prompting architects to use less flammable materials in future constructions and paving the way for greater emphasis on public safety with the introduction of adequate escape routes. From the description of events, it would appear that the electrician had been unfortunate to have been caught up in some terrible replay from the past, witnessing the sounds and sensations from the trapped residual energy. He may even have unwittingly been in the building on the anniversary of the tragedy though this is pure conjecture. We will never know but I do believe that many buildings retain events, particularly tragic ones in their make up, ready to come to life in the right circumstances.

When I got home I was pleasantly surprised to find that I had managed to capture a bright aqua blue anomaly on one of my images, the rest, given the amount of dust in the air was, as you would imagine, covered in pale, transparent dust orbs. I decided to investigate the rumours of an old graveyard but as is often the case I could find no evidence of this, even though I had looked over a number of old maps. I returned some weeks later to catch up with any developments and was told though there had been footsteps heard on occasion generally things were quiet with the work progressing unhindered. A few days later I was pleased to receive the images taken of the wall, containing the 'ghostly faces'. I studied the images and though interesting, are inconclusive. The area, photographed, is full of dust orbs, some of which look like skulls, there are however, a number of faces that do look, under close inspection, like children's faces. They are certainly interesting and may well be paranormal, but equally, the images could be caused by a build up of debris in the air, photographed against a dark wall, which has caused the anomalies. I do believe that some of the workers genuinely experienced something unusual during the renovations; after all it is a very old building. Given the evidence it is equally likely that much of it could be put down to imagination and atmospheric conditions. However, I can personally vouch that I sensed a presence in the basement, but again, as I have experienced, it may have been someone 'popping in' out of curiosity.

Incidentally, the building is situated in close proximity to the former Gordon Place. This now demolished street, which at the turn of the century consisted of a series of ramshackle dwellings, was the setting for a well- documented poltergeist case. The incidents, which occurred in the 1920s, revolved around a ten year old boy, who was thought to have attracted the uninvited presence of a poltergeist. Daily accounts in the local paper kept Aberdonians enthralled for weeks and the story was soon picked up by the national press. The whole country followed the unfolding events, which included details of a number of seances conducted by the local Spiritualist church, in an effort to find out who was responsible. The activity stopped after a number of weeks, and though inconclusive, it was assumed that a recently deceased family member was probably responsible, though others claimed it was the spirit of a suicide, a former neighbour, who was to blame. After the activity stopped, the events became old news and in time people forgot about the Gordon Place poltergeist. The area, long since redeveloped, offers little clue as to how it would have looked at the time of the haunting. It is worth noting however, that acclaimed author and storyteller, Stanley Robertson, himself a 'sensitive', stated that the area always 'gave him the creeps' and had an unpleasant feel to it, he said it was known locally as 'poltergeist alley'

Powis House

Powis House or Powis Community Centre as its known today was built around 1800 by the architect George Jaffray and has had a colourful past from family estate, to library to community centre and is without doubt the most spiritually active building I have ever visited. Again, it is common knowledge among locals and staff as to its reputation and yet has never been written about. There is an air of mystery to the building and also as to the fate of the woman who appears to be the predominant spirit that haunts it. Powis had been described at that time as a 'straggling estate' which is certainly true as it covered a considerable distance from Kittybrewster to Old Aberdeen. The entrance to what was the estate is still marked today by two ornate towers. These stand in the High Street of Old Aberdeen and are known as Powis Gate. Powis as a housing scheme was not to be thought of for over a hundred years. In fact you could have been forgiven for thinking you were in the country, as period etchings show. I first heard about Powis House when I was assisting a student write a local history report. Melissa had chosen the subject of crime and punishment in historic Aberdeen, which was a popular subject among my students. We had inevitably got onto the subject of haunted houses and she mentioned that Powis was well known for its ghost among the local community. She and a close friend had first hand experience of this about ten years previously when as usual they were hanging about outside the building at night which was a meeting place for the local kids. Even though the centre had shut for the night they continued 'muck about' near the building. Her friend Kevin, whose name I have changed, was standing outside when something from inside the building caught his eye. Standing at a window looking out was a female with long dark hair, wearing what appeared to be either a light coloured dress or night gown, the face was pale and the features indistinct. The room in which she stood appeared to have what he described as 'a blue light' inside it, which glowed. The window from which she looked is at the front of the house and distinctive because of its half moon shape and from his vantage point could see her clearly. The figure turned and walked away from the window, the blue light also receding. Melissa at the time was unaware of what he was seeing until she heard him let out a 'scream'. She went to his aid but he tore past her without explanation as to what had happened and bolted for home. She stated that it took her weeks to find out what had happened as 'he refused to leave his house for about a month' and was unwilling to discuss what he had seen. I listened intently as in a strange quirk of fate Kevin had attended one of my classes about two years previously and told me practically the same story. I remembered at the time his demeanour which suggested he was telling the truth and he seemed to have genuinely disturbed by the incident so much so that he did not like talking about it. He told me she had looked at him.

I went home that night intent on telling my partner Carol about Powis House and was surprised to hear that she had also had an experience there around eight years ago which took place in the basement of the building. Having visited the building a number of times I must confess I have felt slightly apprehensive in the basement. It is accessed by a small rounded stairwell, rumoured to be the location where a servant was killed after being shoved down the stairs (incidentally I have found no evidence to back this up). A set of doors leads to a long dim corridor with a series of rooms running off it, some bathrooms, a music room, assorted cupboards and a wash room containing large antiquated washing machines. It was in this room that Carol was loading one of the washing machines and as she stood back waiting for the cycle to begin became aware of an intense feeling of someone standing directly behind her. The hair on her neck stood on end and she bolted, terrified up the stairs and burst into the main office where she recounted her experience. The staff seemed nonplussed and casually said 'that will be Annie' the generic name given by some to the spirit. Being well known for her interactions among staff, Annie has become part of the fabric of the building though no one really knows who she was. I managed with the help of Melissa to arrange a visit and arrived on a bright spring day. Having never seen the building before it was a pleasant surprise. Built in grey granite and over two hundred years old it looked imposing with its columns sparkling in the sunshine. I took a moment to imagine what it must have been like surrounded by grass and trees before the council estate surrounded it and couldn't help but notice the incongruous looking telephone box outside contrasting with its elegant neighbour. I met with one of the community staff and spent some time being shown press clippings relating to the centre, how after the second war it was opened for the community, making it the oldest centre of its kind in Aberdeen. It was also used as a library at one point and my dad who lived on Bedford Road, remembered it as a child and it was apparently quite grand. We sat in the room which used to house the library, and in which the apparition was seen. The room, which incidentally retains its ornate ceiling and cornices featuring relief portraits of the Lesley family is certainly worth seeing alone and I kept having to remind myself that I was in a community centre.

I was then taken to the attic and left to my own devices to take some images, which I did before returning to the main office. I left some questionnaires making a mental note to return in the near future. A few days later I spoke to Melissa at work and asked if she would speak to her grandmother, a former cleaner at the centre. Melissa's grandmother, who by her own admission did not enjoy her work, remembers going to the basement to get the tools of her trade in the evening and having someone mischievously turn out the light, or even worse when she was in the attic, causing her to fumble for the switch. Melissa remembers as a child 'helping grandma' just about every day and now understands why. It was for company as she remembers having her tea there while granny worked. One particular incident stands out from that period, one that was instrumental in her eventually handing in her notice. Melissa was sitting downstairs having a snack, which her mother had dropped off, when she heard a scream coming from upstairs.

She ran upstairs and claims her grandmother was 'pure white'. She had seen the figure of a girl in the attic beside a small door that, although locked, leads to the eaves. It is interesting to note that there is a story concerning the upper part of the house and that when the Leslies resided there, two of their children died at an early age from what was thought to be scarlet fever in the attic rooms, then a nursery. This has not yet been verified but the spirit of a young lady has been seen on a number of occasions, though it would appear there is a connection with children also as she has been seen 'nursing' a child by other witnesses. So who is the spirit person? Sightings have included a woman sometimes with child sometimes not, a young girl and also the disembodied voice of a man. There are a number of suspects. Before I continue with the story it may be worth looking at who we know lived there until its sale to the council in the early 1940s. The home belonged to the Leslie family when newly built till the late 1800s and census entries for that period show the huge amount of residents, both Leslies and their servants who resided there. For example the original owner, Hugh Leslie died leaving the estate to his heir John Leslie of Powis, the eldest son of ten brothers and sisters ranging from a man of twenty years to a child of 15 months. It has been written that two children born just prior to the building of the house, Agnes Anne and Isabella 'died young' possibly while residing their, though no mention of a date is given. The Leslies continued to occupy the house and by now rapidly shrinking estate into the latter part of the century when the University of Aberdeen appeared to buy the property. Directories from the time show that the house was lived in by William Sorley, professor of moral philosophy and for a short while his son Charles Hamilton Sorley the acclaimed war poet who gave his life fighting in the trenches. The building was then rented to a successive number of university staff and it appears, according to a directory, a cattle sales company before being bought by the council in 1941 for use as a community centre and library. The meeting of the council at that time notes 'with reference to the minutes of the council, of date 3rd February last, relative to the transfer of Powis House and an area

146

of ground surrounding it, extending in all to 1.33 acres or thereby, to the education department, a report was submitted by the city assessor fixing the sum to be paid by the education department to the common good for the said subjects at £1,000'.

With all this in mind my colleague Duncan and I decided to approach the community centre staff with a view to taking more photographs and were invited up soon after. We were given the opportunity to walk round and although the building has changed vastly inside there are still glimpses of the past to see. We decided to go up to what was formerly the attic but is now various activity rooms and decided to hold a short meditation in one of the main rooms. As we stood there concentrating I asked in my mind 'if someone is there can you please show yourself'. Almost instantaneously we were surrounded by a cold spot, an indication of spirit and felt the associated tingling sensations. Duncan had also become aware of this and I quickly moved back and took some digital images of the area. The energy followed us around the room for about a minute before moving away. The picture, much to my joy had captured a crescent shaped pink mist at the spot where I had been standing. It was times like this that made up for all those wasted hours capturing nothing but the mandatory dust orbs. Prior to this I had been about to enter one of the small attic rooms, when I was overcome with genuine dread, though I can't explain it, all I knew was that someone was in the room, it made me feel uneasy and yet when I eventually pulled myself together and entered the room it felt light. Before leaving I passed in a number of questionnaires to the office staff. Despite feeling a bit of a nuisance, pestering is sometimes the only way.

Around three weeks later a questionnaire appeared at work and I was pleasantly surprised to find that whoever had filled it in had taken the time to detail their experiences rather that write just yes or no which is a fairly common response, nice but not very helpful due to the all important lack of detail. The questionnaire was from Michael who works part time at the centre where he runs a music project, and as it transpired works mainly from the basement. I phoned him and he described in greater detail a number of events that had taken place in the building around the time of June 2006. Mike takes up the story: "I was in the music room and there were three girls who wanted to record themselves singing. They were about to start, walked up to the microphone, opened their mouths but before they could make a sound a male voice boomed out through the speaker. I couldn't understand what he was saying but he spoke for a few seconds. The girls screamed and were upset though I calmed them down by saying it was a passing taxi driver being picked up, though really I don't think the equipment is capable of doing this." This was nothing to what happened on the 24th of July 2006 when Mike was in the building moving the contents of the music room out for a gala day at Hilton. His colleague was elsewhere in the building and Mike, while stacking amplifiers in one of the family rooms, became aware of something in the air behind him. Turning quickly he saw 'the ghost of a woman in front of me, she had a white dress and appeared to be nursing a baby'. She was in the corner by the door and he described how the image of the woman appeared to come together with a 'whoosh' before dissolving back into nothing in a few seconds. Despite the sudden appearance of the woman, he felt 'quite calm, almost peaceful'. Michael, who always looks for a rational explanation cannot find one, and when the amplifiers started playing up again he went as far as to take speakers back to the shop to be checked over. I decided after we had finished the conversation to contact the centre in the next few months, and when doing so Michael suggested we carry out a 'little experiment'. Life caught up and with work taking precedence it was January 2007 before I had the opportunity to meet him again. When we eventually met he told me about the number of incidents that had occurred since we spoke last, one concerning the heater in the music room which kept being switched on. This was verified by community worker Suzy, who stated the heating had been switched on regularly when the room was locked and on one occasion had only been discovered when a week later the room was opened up for classes. The build up of heat was incredible and was causing concern not only for the damage it could cause to the equipment but also as it posed a serious fire risk. She was aware that this had happened once before when staff had forgotten it was left on, but had spoken to the staff concerned and everyone since then had made sure it was switched off. The room was always locked, only specific staff being designated key holders and no one could explain who or what was doing this. It was also mentioned by staff in the office that recently someone was heard walking up the main staircase to the attic and when they went up to investigate who was in the building there was no one there. With slight trepidation we first went to the room where the figure had appeared. Michael suggested that we turn the lights off, while he stood at the spot where the spirit had manifested itself. I stood at the exact spot where he had been and waited. After less than a minute he mentioned he was starting to feel something in the air, a change in the atmosphere and at this point I started to take shots with the digital camera. On the screen next to Michael was a large bright white orb, which looked like a floating dinner plate. I took some more shots and standing next to Michael instantly felt the same cold sensation. The atmosphere was electric and lasted for another twenty seconds or thereabouts. We looked over the images noting another orb, which was transparent and appeared to have moved a few feet away from where he was standing. Continuing we ventured down to the basement and searched the rooms, even setting up the equipment to simulate previous events though nothing came through. It was at this point that he recounted an incident that had happened four weeks previously, witnessed by three other band members. Michael takes up the story: "We were in the music room with the band in full swing when we heard an enormous crash in the corridor outside. Putting down the instruments we ran outside and saw the fire extinguisher on the floor, it was still rolling. On investigating, we saw the pin at the top was completely bent. The strangest thing was that it would have to have been lifted off the bracket, upended then dropped to have caused the damage. We were pretty shook up as the noise was so loud it could be heard over the guitars and the door was shut at the time." We looked at the replacement extinguisher and he pointed out the brackets, which he correctly observed would have held it securely unless it was manually lifted off. John, head of establishment was equally perplexed as there was no one else in the building at the time of the incident and subsequently had to replace it. We spent some more time in the basement, though nothing unusual happened and eventually decided to head back upstairs. After hearing a noise on the floor above we locked up quickly and ascended the stairs but were pleasantly surprised and a little relieved to find the cleaner who on hearing us on the stair remarked: "I thought it was the ghost." I was told later that she refuses to go to the basement on her own. We parted company though I promised to continue to visit Powis periodically to see if any further phenomena occurred. It was in February in 2007 that I received further news from Powis again concerning EVP. Michael takes up the story: "I had set up some recording equipment for to girls to record a song they had been practising. I had to leave them for two minutes with my assistant in charge whilst I went upstairs to do some photocopying (neither of the girls nor my assistant had any knowledge of my 'trouble' with the speakers). No sooner had I reached the upstairs room when both girls and my assistant came running and screaming out of the music room. They said that a voice shouted at them through the speakers and began making breathing noises. They were all very upset and shaken and refused to go back in there. I went to see if there was anything wrong with the equipment but it was as quiet as I had left it, ready to record."

The building though obviously active still holds on to its mysteries and at present I am left with a number of unanswered questions, mainly who are the spirit people who reside there? My theory is that like many other old buildings there is an accumulation of energy built up over time. It would, I imagine, have to be someone with a connection to the Leslie family either family member or servant and looking at the census of the time reveals a number of possibilities including maids and other general help. There are also a number of tales associated with the property including three different tragedies which supposedly took place. These have been mentioned by both staff and locals who have used the centre over the years and include the two children who died through illness, the female who was supposedly pushed down stairs or in other versions took her own life after an affair with one of the Leslies. All have been submitted as reasons for the activity, though none were able to verify it. These stories, it appears, have been around for years and have been passed by word of mouth since who knows when though there is a fair chance of there being a grain of truth in them. During my research I discovered that at least three of the Leslie children died very young and were known to have resided in 'powies' though there is a little discrepancy in the dates between their deaths and that of the building's completion. There is also an obvious male presence who has let himself be known on a number of occasions by using the recording equipment as a means of communication. I can personally verify that there is definite spirit activity within the building and is very intense at times, but who causes it remains open to speculation. I spent some time looking through the old census records and could not find anyone of the name Annie associated with the building though that does not necessarily mean she did not exist. As is often the case in past times a possible scandal could easily have been covered up through fair means or foul, servants after all were unfortunately 'expendable'. In conclusion I was told that a person with mediumistic abilities visited the building some years ago who was able to link with spirit and claimed that the 'owners' had been upset by all the people using their building but now accepted it. The building itself remains stoic in its 'new' surroundings. A popular focal point, it has served the community for many years. Despite the shared premises the consensus among most people appears to be that they have 'learned to live with it' and 'the atmosphere is mostly pleasant."

The Ghosts That Never Were

When I was young I liked nothing better than settling down in bed with a ghost book. Factual or fictional it did not really matter, the accompanying thrill was what I was after, though in retrospect these 'thrills' caused no end of sleepless nights. The otherworldly proved endlessly fascinating to me. I was particularly drawn to those set in the Victorian, Edwardian era, where good manners were always a requisite to a weekend stay in the country house run by an old friend from Eton. The friend unfortunately due to some unnamed malady had usually aged. I knew the reason why and eagerly awaited the denouement. It was during this era that I became acquainted with the work of Eliott O' Donnell the self styled ghost hunter of the Victorian/Edwardian era who wrote prolifically on the subject. Born in Ireland he spent a great deal of his life touring Britain, writing countless articles on the supernatural. He had many friends and was continually invited, well at least according to his books, to stay anywhere there appeared to be a restless spirit. His books fascinated me as he continually appeared to suffer from the most horrific visitations from beyond, prompting that great writer of the supernatural M.R.James to tartly remark: "I sincerely hoped the ghosts described by O' Donnell were fictional, since life might otherwise become an extremely hazardous business."

The real draw for me however was that he had spent some time in Aberdeen in the early 1900s and his experiences of those times were recorded for posterity. But the question remains, were they based on real events? I totally accepted them as a child, at the age when your imagination is at its most vivid, and the fact that I lived near one of the supposed locations added to the mystery. I would shudder involuntarily as I walked down the street, wondering which house might be the haunted one until one day it dawned on me that it was described as being long gone.

Undaunted I would then try to imagine where it had stood and so this continued 'till adulthood.

Doubt as to its authenticity began to manifest as I grew older and during my research I began the logical process of looking for evidence. I wanted to know where these haunted houses were, and if in fact they ever existed. It was and is still not my intention to attempt to besmirch anyone's name by questioning their integrity. However I began to realise how important it is during serious research, to separate fact from fiction, and so decided to pursue this further. As mentioned he wrote and had published countless articles on the subject but interestingly never allowed anyone within the burgeoning field of parapsychology to investigate his claims. In fact it has been recorded that he studiously avoided this. He also decried spiritualism which to me is nonsensical as one of their basic principles is the belief in continuing life. Being that he had more encounters with spirit than seems feasible, I began to wonder what made him tick. He may not have wanted to be part of an 'organised religion', which I can appreciate and given the complexity of his character it comes as no surprise. It was revealed by his writing that he had a dual nature, having a strong belief in the superstitions rife in his homeland coupled with a more analytical side. Such was his continuing popularity, even after death, that the 'Evening Express' ran a series of articles, recounting his exploits in Aberdeen circa 1900, which appeared in the 1960s. I read them with great interest, able to recognise the areas in which he had stayed. One made mention of an alleged haunting in a house in the region of the Shiprow in which he stayed overnight. He apparently suffered a frightening visitation and was able to tell the owners of the possible source. But herein lies the problem, tantalising though it was, in his description of events, there was no detail. I wanted to know who owned the house, where exactly on Shiprow was it located, it was all so vague. In fact he never gave accurate details when recounting his adventures preferring names of houses and people to be omitted, to save the protagonists modesty or at least that was the excuse used. As there were a number of cases relating to Aberdeen I decided to concentrate on two of his best known, those being of an apparent suicide in the region of Great Western Road and also perhaps his most widely read tale, which crops up with great regularity, 'The White Dove Hotel' or the 'Hindu child' as its sometimes known. This particular tale has been reprinted in numerous ghost books and in all those books not one person has ever questioned it's authenticity, which I find staggering.

This story was told to him, by a nurse who was engaged to look after an ailing actress residing at the hotel. The address was given as either St.Swithin Street or in the vicinity of, depending on the version and was described as an old building which no longer stands suggesting it was possibly of the Georgian period. The date of the incident was given as early 1900s. According to the story the nurse in question was subjected to visitations by the apparition of a young girl while she tended to her patient, Miss Vinning. The young girl eventually revealed herself to be a corpse much to the horror of the nurse. The patient, former actress Miss Vinning who was suffering from an unspecified malady, passed away at that very moment. The story, though gripping, is in my opinion, a work of fiction, albeit a good one.

My first port of call was the local studies department of the reference library where I looked through their Post Office directories which list home owners, occupations and businesses from that period. I found, after many days, nothing in or around the area that could have been a possible location. Undaunted I contacted the city council, who despite having one of the most comprehensive archives in the country, were unable to find any hotels remotely matching the description from the period. Given that St.Swithin Street itself had been built a number of years before the events supposedly took place, it gave credence to the fact it most likely never existed. Even with the possibility of a name change there did not appear to be a match. Out of frustration I went to the births, deaths and marriages record office to search for the name Vinning and it came as no surprise that there were no records of anyone of that name. I then paid for an assisted search on the database for the name Ann Webb, another restless spirit in Eliot O' Donnell's canon. She was named as the tragic suicide in the second story, returning from beyond to protest her innocence in a case of wrongful fraud. This story was cited as occurring in Great Western Road around the early 1900's and again involved someone else rather than the author as the main protagonist. I went through the same search as before and as suspected found no evidence to back up the story. What left me feeling deflated was the realisation that the stories I grew up with were works of fiction and so the mystique was destroyed. Eliot O' Donnell may well have had paranormal experiences in his life, he was certainly regarded as an expert by many and had influential friends who appeared more than happy to allow him to investigate their properties. Unfortunately, given that the aforementioned tales are fictitious, it casts doubt on all his other supposed true stories. In a last ditch effort to be proved wrong I contacted the Maryland Library where they hold the O' Donnell archives in which his exploits in Aberdeen were allegedly recorded. I hoped to have my faith restored by new information though remained doubtful. Some time later I was contacted by the archivist who having searched the memoirs could find no reference to the White Dove Hotel or indeed Aberdeen. Though disappointed and despite the fact these stories were fictional we shouldn't forget he was a great storyteller and they will undoubtedly be enjoyed by generations to come, though please take them with a large pinch of salt.

A Torry Timeslip

The definition of a time slip is described as an alleged paranormal incident in which a person, or group of people travel through time through supernatural means, witnessing scenes from the past. Though there have been many reported cases from individuals and groups witnessing battles, replays of marching armies there has, in most cases, been no direct interaction. However this is not always the case as in the 'Ghosts of Versailles' case of 1901. This case involved two respected academics, Anne Elizabeth Moberly and Eleanor Frances Jourdain the Principal and Vice Principal of St. Hugh's College, Oxford who believed they had been caught up in a time slip which transported them back to the time of the French revolution.

On August 10th 1901 Moberly and Jourdain were visiting the Palace of Versailles and were strolling in the grounds when they became aware of a feeling of oppressive gloom. They encountered and interacted with a number of people being described as wearing old fashion clothing as well a sighting someone who was thought to be Marie Antoinette. Critics of the story claimed that Marie Antoinette was not present at that time in Versailles and it was more likely to have been friends of the French poet Robert De Montesquiou who were known to dress up in period costume and give parties for charity. Others argued that this could not be the case as the story was not revealed till after the death of Ms. Jourdain in 1924 therefore ruling out a publicity stunt and that admitting to an incident of this nature would have been tantamount to professional suicide for the pair. Ms. Moberly's account was rich in detail describing that an extraordinary depression came over her and the surrounding gardens began to look unnatural with trees appearing 'flat and lifeless' and that the air became 'intensely still', a feeling that appears to accompany many times slips, with sound becoming muted or ceasing completely.

Other time slip stories involve witnesses to full scale battles, marching armies, agricultural scenes from a different age and in a widely publicised case from 1979 the disappearance of a hotel. This particular tale involved two English married couples who came across an old-fashioned hotel while driving through France en route to Spain. They stayed the night and decided to stop over at the same hotel on the return leg of their journey. Their plans changed when they were unable to find the hotel and photographs taken during their initial stay were found to be missing despite being in the middle of a roll of film. The phenomena of the time slip tends to share common factors these being that surroundings appear flat and lifeless, sound appears muffled and there is usually an accompanying feeling of unease or depression. Reports vary as to whether those experiencing time slips can take an active part in the event. In the case of the Versailles ghost story it would appear so, as with the holidaymakers who went one step further and ate dinner and breakfast during their 'visit'. In other reported incidents the witness is usually a passive observer of the event replaying which tends to last for only a few minutes. The following two incidents occurred much closer to home at the Torry Point Battery and during one in particular, the unwitting subjects literally wandered into a scene from the past.

The Torry Battery, with its unparalleled views of Aberdeen bay, was initially built between 1859 and 1861 as a defence against possible attack from France. Though ultimately never seeing action during that period its defences included 200lb Armstrong guns capable of 'dropping a ball from Torry as far as Newburgh'. Despite the fearsome weaponry the battery was mainly used as a training ground for soldiers. It served this purpose until the end of World War One when a desperate housing shortage helped shape its destiny of the next twenty years. With many troops returning home to poverty and no chance of housing, the Battery, though not ideal, at least provided temporary respite for the homeless. The building's usage changed with the onset of World War Two and returned to its former purpose. As the threat of invasion loomed the now manned defences saw action during the subsequent enemy raids. At the end of the conflict Britain once again faced a stark housing shortage and it was not long before a number of homeless families began squatting at the site. The City Council realising the magnitude of the problem formalised a plan to allow families to take up residency in an array of huts and outbuildings where despite basic amenities there was a great sense of community. This situation lasted until 1953 when the last occupants moved out, beginning a period of decline for the Battery. Despite erosion, vandalism and the removal of buildings the shell of the Battery still stands and is now recognised as a place of natural heritage, home to many rare species of bird.

I recently met with adult learner Connie, who told me the following tale, involving her mother. In the late 1960s her mother, Sandra, and her friends, all bikers, were witness to events at the Torry Battery and subsequently the Duthie Park which were very frightening and unexplainable. Her mother takes up the story: "It was a summers evening in 1968 at approximately 10pm. There were four of us, on two motorbikes, and we decided to stop at the Battery for a ciggie. We drove in the gate and parked beside two cellars. We were standing next to the bikes and chatted for about 15 minutes when two young women entered the gate in front of us. We all saw them and in fact I said to them, jokingly, to watch out for the ghosties. They both then turned and stared directly at me for what seemed like ages, a cold stare that went right through me. They never said a word and turned and walked away from us to the back of the Battery. We all started talking about their strange behaviour, and as the girls disappeared over a large mound, one of the guys, who had been to the Battery before, said, he wondered where they were going as there was no way out that way. We decided to follow them as it was beginning to get dark and we were very puzzled. We looked over the mounds and in the out buildings, which were in ruins. But we could not find them. We decided to get on our bikes and go round behind the Battery, which in those days was walled and had barbed wire round it, though there was still no sign of them". The four friends, by now slightly unnerved decide to leave at that point and headed back into town. Sandra continued. "We then decided to go to the Duthie Park. The guys parked their motorbikes in the shelter, chaining their front wheels together and we went to the duck pond, where we sat chatting and having a ciggie. It was around 11pm. We had only been there a matter of minutes when we heard motorbikes revving. Hughie, my boyfriend, immediately recognised his bikes engine and we all ran back towards the shelter. When we got there both bikes were lying on their side, the chain connecting them had been snapped, not cut, and all the wheels were spinning. Everyone was frightened, including the guys. They had their keys in their pockets and we got the bikes and took off. A few weeks later, while discussing the matter, two different people told us that after WW2, two young girls had been found murdered, on a mattress, in one of the cellars at the Battery." Sandra finished of by saying: "All of us believed the incident was paranormal, and we never went back."

I was indebted to Sandra for recounting this tale, as it was not the first account I had heard about the Battery, as you will read.

In January 2008, I had been taking photographs of a building during refurbishment and had got chatting to site manager, Ian. In the course of the conversation he told me of an incident that had happened to some friends, in the 1990s, also at the Torry Battery. This incident, like Sandra's, again involved a sighting of a number of figures. Having hurriedly scribbled some notes, I returned home and after perusing them I realised that I was missing some important pieces of information. I promised myself to return and some months later, after receiving Sandra's story, I again, met up with Ian. As we sat in the bothy, I began by asking him to recount the story. He began to speak in greater detail about the incident and on finding out that I was taking the subject seriously admitted that he had also been there that night, though like many others, had been reticent to say to much for fear of being laughed at. I assured him that I was taking his story seriously and mentioned that I had also recently received a further account from a lady, who used to be a biker. The only other worker in the bothy, Ben, immediately spoke up, and asked if the ladies name was Sandra. I confirmed it was. As it transpired, Sandra was a close friend's grandmother, and once our collective jaws had been picked of the floor we marvelled at how fate had again played its hand in providing back up. Ben was well aware of the 'motor bike incident', having heard the story on a number of occasions from his friend. Ian seemed genuinely surprised that his co-worker was party to the story and very soon began to tell his tale from the beginning. I have been given permission to repeat this in full.

"It was in the summer of 1995 and I was an apprentice at the time. We used to meet down at the breakwater near the mouth of the harbour and stay out playing football and having parties. On this night, there were three of us heading towards the breakwater, myself and my two mates, Kevin Porter and Alan Black. It was a perfect night in the height of summer, no breeze and still hot. It was starting to turn dark, and as we were running late someone suggested cutting through the Battery. We were cutting through the Battery when out of the corner of my eye, I noticed Alan looking at something. We were stopped in our tracks by the sight of a group of people wearing old-fashioned clothing like out of the television programme Foyles War. There were a number of women wearing long dresses, just standing there, and a soldier standing nearby, wearing army greens and a cap. There were others wearing flat caps. We were rooted to the spot and though, I suppose, it only lasted seconds, time seemed to stand still. It was surreal and though not exactly frightening. The air was perfectly calm and I felt at peace. The strangest thing was that there were also children playing, and one wee boy, wearing what looked like plus fours, and of Asian appearance was running along with a hope which he was directing with a stick. Like an old fashioned toy. The only noise I could hear was the sound of the hoop rattling on the ground and the stick hitting it. We looked at each other and bolted through the Battery, over the other side and ran all the way to where our mates were. When we arrived we were breathless and my friends looked pale. When we told the rest what had happened they laughed and thought we were winding them up. After some persuasion, they agreed to come back with us and we headed back quickly. Between us running to our mates and returning, must have only taken around ten minutes, but when we got to the Battery the place was deserted. There was no sign of life, not even a crisp packet on the ground, silent. My mates continued to dispute what we saw, claiming that it must have been someone making a film. They did not believe us, but we knew it wasn't a film set, as there were no cars or vans there, nowhere for anyone to go. There is no way they could have cleared the place out in the ten minutes it took to return. The experience has stuck with me and felt more surreal and peaceful than frightening though were alarmed to an extent."

I got ready to leave and thanked Ian for his time, and for recalling the story in such detail. He was interested to hear of Sandra's experience and likewise believed it was something of paranormal origin, though what exactly remains a mystery to him. Afterwards I spent some time researching the Battery, but could find no evidence to support the story of the murdered women, despite searching the newspapers of the period. Perhaps this element was an urban myth, a rumour, however I believe that after experiencing something of this nature it is only natural to seek explanations and it is amazing the variety of theories put forward by others. The fact that there appeared to be an element of interaction between Sandra's group and the two young women is unusual and would suggest a visitation rather than a recording. In respect of Ian's story, in particular, It is known, that a number of families did live there after both wars, and up till the 1950s. The centre of the Battery was a place where people met and children played and perhaps the best explanation for his experience is that of being caught up in a recording from the past.

The Battery remains a popular attraction to this day with bird watchers, photographers and locals out for a bracing walk, but I wonder how many people would care to wander up there, when all is quite and the visitors have gone home?

Rosemount Community Centre

The community centre started life in the late 19th century as Rosemount Secondary School before becoming the annexe of the Aberdeen Grammar School. Situated near a number of Victorian villas, the school took in a large population of children who 'swarm in the locality,' as was described in a newspaper article of 1897. The building is, as you would expect from the Victorian era, a formidable granite structure, which eventually incorporated the nearby villas, as a means of coping with the expanding population. Not every one was happy with the idea of expansion however. With the possibility of overcrowding at the time being cited as a possible death trap, due in no small part to narrow stairs, objections to a number of new proposals were publicly aired in some quarters. The proposal to build a fourth floor met with further resistance, and in an article from the Aberdeen Journal the scheme was described as a 'fantastic and mischievous proposal.' The author's acidic pen went further describing the proposal to add a fourth floor as 'an emanation from the fertile brain of Mr. Hugh F. Campbell' (presumably someone on the school board or the architect) and that 'the man who proposes such a scheme deserves to be drummed out of Aberdeen.' Whether he ever did remains a mystery. Despite this the school continued to flourish through two world wars, with an intake of around 800 pupils recorded at its peak.

In later years the building served as an annexe to its neighbour the Grammar School before being used as a community centre, where to this day it serves the local population by providing training and support for a diverse range of groups. It was during my support of one particular group that I first became aware of the stories circulating among staff as to the possible presence of a spirit and I wasted no time in trying to find out more, being regaled with a number of diverse, eyewitness accounts.

The activity, in this building, ranges from people having the sensation of being followed to full figure manifestations, with the lights being tampered with on occasion, for good measure. I met with community workers, Lil and Fiona who were kind enough to take the time to explain some of their experiences associated with the building. Though neither had personally seen anything, Lil was keen to point out that when she works in a particular classroom, she is aware of a 'spooky feeling' and does not like the atmosphere. She went on to explain that a number of staff have felt like they were being followed, and on turning have been faced with an empty corridor. The building itself is large with a maze of corridors and stairways and it was verified that on particular occasions, the lights are tampered with, being switched back on when there is no one about. More sceptical members of the staff, put this down to the age of the wiring, though others believe it to be paranormal. Although they concurred that incidents like these are more annoying than frightening, as if someone had been playing a prank. This theory is backed up by the frequent disappearance and movement of paperwork and office equipment, which would then be found, 'where it shouldn't be.' Slightly more unnerving for some, were the unaccounted footsteps heard busily walking down the corridor, usually when there was a lone member of staff working. During the conversation, Lil pointed out that 'furniture has also been moved in the night' with cleaners adamant it was not of their doing.

After our conversation, I was taken for a tour of the building in which I had spent a number of years there, as a pupil myself, then still an annexe of Aberdeen Grammar School. It felt strange to be walking along vaguely familiar corridors and the memories began to flood back, though my recollection was still somewhat foggy. During the tour I had the opportunity to visit the old assembly hall with its shiny parquet flooring, scene of one of the 'light tampering' incidents. Fiona stated: "That this particular area was one where she had felt 'watched' on occasion." And she did not enjoy being there on her own. I did not feel anything untoward and was lost in reverie at the sight and smell of the room, the latter being most prominent, with that peculiar odour that seems to be inextricably linked to parquet flooring, overpowering. When we had finished, I was asked to leave some questionnaires behind as two absent staff members had particularly interesting experiences to relate.

Some weeks later I returned and met with Frances, who works in the community office. During our meeting, she explained that early one morning before usual opening time, she was sitting at her desk when she caught a glimpse of something near the office door. Glancing up she was confronted by a 'solid, real looking figure of a woman of African appearance'. She noticed that the women was looking around, and assuming she was waiting for the crèche to open, put her head down and went back to work. Noticing movement, she looked up again and saw the woman heading towards the staff toilet. She waited for the woman to return. Minutes past and still she did not return. Wondering if there was some kind of problem, Frances got up and went into the toilets to see if the visitor was okay. She was shocked to find that they were completely empty and all the windows locked, affording no possible means of escape. Where she went to remains a mystery as from her desk she had a very clear view of the bathroom, situated only a matter of feet from her desk. On being asked what she thought about the incident, Frances replied, "I am not normally a believer, but what happened on that day left me shaken." I asked to see the room, and was shown the toilets, noticing, that despite the windows, there was no way anyone could have got out had they tried, due to their size and position. Frances went on to say that: "it is quite usual to hear doors closing and footsteps in corridors, even when I am alone in the building or the outside doors are locked and staff accounted for." In conclusion she mentioned that it is common for switches to be 'interfered with' in the toilet area, heaters get turned off and items go missing. To find out more, I was told I should speak to her colleague Averil.

Soon after, I had the opportunity to speak to her by phone and asked about her experiences during her tenure at the community centre. She was particularly interested in Frances's story as she explained that she had seen a figure in the same area a few years previously. I asked what time in the morning did the incident occur and where, she replied before opening time, and in the corridor next to the toilets. She described, how she noticed a female figure moving along the corridor, past the office, and on seeing it, went out to ask if she could help, only to find it empty. She described to me, that the figure appeared to be wearing 'something coloured red', perhaps a cape, but was moving to quickly to ascertain exactly what. Being perturbed by the incident, she spoke to a colleague, who said the description of the clothing, could possibly have been that of a Red Cross nurse, as they were known to have a worn red cape, or at least, they were thought, to have had a red insignia on it. As if this was not enough, some time later a further incident occurred. It was wintertime on a Saturday night at 6.30, and dark. Averil and a youth worker had just finished working with a group and after switching off the lights and locking up the building, were in the car park about to leave. They were both surprised to see the lights in the old assembly hall and corridor suddenly come on, and she concluded by saying; "We never went to investigate."

I have not had the opportunity to fully look into this particular building's history, though I intend to gather more information as it presents itself. Staff still claim to sense a foreboding atmosphere at times, a feeling of being watched, which is most prevalent in the old assembly hall and in the main first floor corridor. From what little I know it appears that the building was used as a Red Cross hospital during World War One, and that someone has suggested that the old assembly hall was used as a morgue. This remains speculation, but there would definitely have been patients and more importantly nurses there at the time. Perhaps more puzzling is Frances's experience, as the figure appeared solid and wore contemporary clothing. Perhaps she was someone recently passed, connected to the centre? We may never know.

View Terrace

This former dwelling was built in 1872 by architect George Brown, and was initially known as View Place House. One of the first houses in this particular street, its first residents enjoyed a certain level of privacy with old maps of the period showing a curved sweeping drive and large garden to front and back. The granite, pillared structure was one of many of its ilk throughout the city but as is the case with expansion many were lost when formal rows of tenements were set out during the late Victorian era. Notable first owners included the Reverend John Mearns in 1885 and the Reverend J. Stewart of the North United Free Church. It was also known to have been a 'boarding establishment' in 1888 run by a Mrs. W. Gillanders. By 1911 it become known as View House, and remained thus until the 1940s when it became a pre-school day care centre.

Due to the buildings current usage I was unable to personally visit but the following was related to me, by former employee Anne and involved not only her but a number of colleagues. As with many of the cases I have looked at, I have taken the information in good faith and as I know the main eyewitness well, I can personally vouch for her integrity. Anne worked in the building for over ten years between March 1989 and April 2000 and what follows is a series of incidents recorded over that period. When we met to discuss the following, Anne immediately mentioned, that 'staff had always spoke about things being moved and about the green lady', a generic term, though one that is at least attempting to personalise a spirit. I suggested that perhaps this is in lieu of truly knowing who that person was in this life, and that it is a very common description among many eyewitnesses when there is a lack of information. Anne was aware, also, that when she first joined the team this was one of the first things that was mentioned, as incidents in the building had certainly been ongoing before her employment. Perhaps one of the most common occurrences, and one that took place fairly early on, was the sound of singing that was heard, especially first thing in the morning and it must be pointed out that on these occasions all staff were accounted for. Anne explained that: "Sheila (the cook) and I were often just in the building ourselves, when I would hear someone singing (a woman's voice) but on searching the building, there was no-one there." The singing came from the ground floor (there were three levels to the building with an attic area attached to the side of the house.) When asked what she had felt at the time, she replied: "We never felt frightened and I used to call out good morning as we came in, to let her know we had arrived."

Some time later Jenny, the kitchen assistant, approached colleagues after seeing the spirit of a young woman. Anne recounted: "Jenny spoke to us at length of an experience she had when she was opening up the building one morning, but I only found this out later after having seen her myself. It was early and as she approached the building she stated that she noticed a woman's face at the window, looking out. The figure was there long enough for her to provide a vivid description. She was described as being in her thirties with fair coloured hair, hanging loose in ringlets, wearing a light coloured dress." It transpired that Anne did not know any of these details.

People were generally very busy in the building and though rumours continued to circulate among staff, it was not a subject people had the time to dwell on. Anne gave it little thought until one day, while working in the kitchen, a particular incident of note took place. Anne recounted that on this particular day, "I was busy, but hearing a noise, I turned round and noticed a woman with light coloured hair, wearing a beige two-piece outfit, with beads round her neck. She walked through the laundry room with a cup in her hand, which appeared to be delicate, like bone china. I could see her clearly through the open door and on saying hello, she turned and smiled back. I thought at the time she had come from the parent's room and was going to the urn to get water for her tea or coffee. I went through to where she was to introduce myself, thinking she was new parent, but there was no -one there. I was taken aback, and when I described her to my colleague,

Jenny, she told me that she had seen someone fitting that description, looking at her form the kitchen window. We were both stunned.

This however, was not the end of the matter. Some years later, and with the building's closure pending, Anne recalled. "In the top floor of the house, there was a small room on the right, which had previously, in years gone by, been the milk room, where babies bottles were made up and babies were fed. It was now used as a cupboard for storing toys. One afternoon, a group of us were standing outside the office, which was on that floor too, chatting about the closure and the move, when suddenly boxes of Lego and Sticklebricks came flying off the shelves, onto the floor with an almighty crash. We jumped and after recovering could not understand how this could happen, as the shelves were very deep and the boxes stacked correctly. We thought that it may have been the Green Lady, upset at our conversation about the closure. When, we eventually moved to Ashgrove, the strange occurrences appeared to continue, with presumed missing files turning up unexpectedly and being found on our desks as if placed there. Our paperwork was checked thoroughly before the move and we knew that some of these should not have been there."

As we chatted further, it appeared that current staff have found their new workplace to be a 'sick' building due to the amount of people falling ill, with most of the ex View Terrace staff being retired on medical grounds. Anne was not sure why this was the case, but some think that perhaps, whoever was resident in View Terrace has followed them. I found the conversation intriguing, with Anne mentioning that she had heard that the house in View Terrace had belonged to a doctor, and there had been vague stories circulated about an 'affair, with a baby involved, and the possibility of a fire.' Without further detail I had to leave this story as it was and thanked Anne for her time. In the proceeding days and after a brief search in the local library I was pleased to find evidence that a Dr. P. Stewart had lived there in 1930, and continuing to look through the directory, I further noticed that in 1923 a Mrs. Stewart had also resided there. My mind was alive with all sorts of scenarios, probably misplaced, but nevertheless, I wondered if they were husband and wife, and if so, why was his name not in the 1923 directory? My train of thought was interrupted, a few days later with the arrival of a well timed e-mail from Anne, which depending on your point of view, solved part of the mystery or conversely added to it. Unbeknown to her, she had met up with a former employee, based at View Terrace in the early 1970s. They had been chatting generally and the subject of work had come up. Both were amazed at the coincidence, and were soon recounting work experiences including the stories about the 'Green Lady'. It turned out that the lady in question had been witness to a number of strange events herself and explained that one time, as she was about to go home, she could not find her house keys, despite a thorough search. She thought her colleague had hidden them for a joke and questioned her about this. The colleague protested her innocence and in the middle of the conversation the keys came 'hurtling down beside them from out of nowhere.' It 'freaked her and her colleague out'. The former employee also stated that as far a she knew the 'Green Lady' was allegedly once a cook at View Terrace house and she 'had died in a gas explosion, in the kitchen, which took off her arm.' Whether there is any substance to these stories is up to individual belief, however, I am quite prepared to believe that it is possible, and certainly the continued rumours of death due to a fire, or explosion seem even more likely now. As yet I have not been able to verify these facts but as with others I intend to try to.

Kinnaird Head Lighthouse

Kinnaird Head lighthouse in Fraserburgh was the first lighthouse built on mainland Scotland and now home to the Museum of Scottish Lighthouses. The lighthouse was purchased from the Fraser family in 1787 being converted from a sixteenth castle keep. Robert Stevenson, whose name is synonymous with Scottish Lighthouse design, improved the building in 1824 by building a tower within the existing keep. This construction was originally used as living quarters and to house the largest type of lighthouse lens that was ever made. Outside the keep, there are a number of more contemporary buildings nearby, including lighthouse keepers' cottages the latest built in 1902. Popular with tourists, the museum and cottages now hold a vast collection of Scottish lighthouse artifacts, including a number of rooms dedicated to the keepers' lives up until the point when the practice of manning these ceased.

Kinnaird Head has also a number of stories and legends attached to it particularly that of a phantom piper and the alleged haunting of the nearby Wine Tower. Though perhaps not directly linked to the story I have been looking at, the legend of the Kinnaird castle ghost is certainly worth repeating. The Wine Tower itself, remains something of a mystery, though cited as being built around 1570 by Sir Alexander Fraser, its original purpose remains a point of debate. The tower stands around 50 yards from the lighthouse museum on the edge of an outcrop of rock and is allegedly built directly above a 30 metre long cave known as Selches Hole. The entrance to this building, now locked, is on the second floor with entry being gained by a ladder. Though I have not personally seen the inside of the tower, the ladder apparently leads to a second floor vaulted chamber, containing a number of heraldic motifs associated with the Fraser family.

The legend surrounding the Wine Tower, concerns Sir Alexander Frasers' daughter Isobel who incurred the wrath of her father by having a dalliance with a piper of lowly stock. The enraged father forbade the union, locking Isobel in her room. The piper was then taken to Selches Hole and chained up inside, where on the next day, Fraser intended to dissuade him from continuing the romance. In the morning with Isobel at his side, Fraser approached the cave, though unbeknownst to him, during a particularly stormy night the cave had flooded leaving the unfortunate piper dead. In despair Isobel fled from the terrible scene, and climbing the Wine Tower threw herself to her death on the rocks below. Subsequently, on stormy nights, the sound of piping has been reported being heard, coming from the cave, while a figure has been seen wandering the stretch of coast between the castle and the Wine Tower. This tale like many of its kind with its theme of doomed romance and tragedy appears somewhat fanciful in the cold light of day, and oddly quaint in modern times. I personally do not know how much of this is based on real events, or is merely the product of generations of exaggerated storytelling. There is certainly little contemporary evidence to support the story, and no eyewitness accounts of recent times have cast any new light on the legend. I spoke to a former coastguard about this recently, and he indicated that although there is a cave there, it is far smaller than the legend suggests, being around twenty-five foot in length. The cave, according to a local historian was apparently used by the 'Rattray Pirates' to store illicit rum, before being sold on under the watchful eye of the complicit Laird.

Perhaps, without the same resonance as the phantom piper, there are thought to be a number of other spirits at Kinnaird Head. Spirits whose existence appears to be rooted more firmly in fact due to extant reports. The presence of these people have been felt on numerous occasions by both museum staff and ex lighthouse keepers in a number of diverse locations, such as the old keepers cottages, the lighthouse itself and in the café area.

The cottages, now hold an archive of old photographs and uniforms from its time as staff accommodation and initially I thought, as you might suspect, that the spirit is that of a former keeper, however there is at this time no evidence to suggest this. I first became aware of the stories behind Kinnaird when I met with a student, Jane, who had studied the area as part of a college project. The history of the area is fascinating, though I was particularly drawn to the description of a number of alleged paranormal incidents. It appeared that certain visitors to the museum had experienced the feeling of being watched and had noticed rapid temperature drops, particularly, in and around the lighthouse. Intrigued, I asked permission to speak to some of the people involved and meeting up with Jane, soon found myself at Kinnaird, wandering around the grounds of the Lighthouse complex, in the hope of finding out more. We decided to walk the museum trail and soon found ourselves in one of the former keepers' cottages, now housing lighthouse memorabilia. Jane, having previously experienced something unusual in the kitchen of the building, on a prior visit, immediately took me there. On entering the room we were stopped in our tracks by the atmosphere that greeted us. It was apparent that there was someone there, a female, who we felt was surprised to see us. Our hair stood on end and as we put out our hands, we could feel the energy moving around us. Standing in the incongruous surroundings of the 1970s kitchen, and with the bright noon day sun beaming in, we continued to follow the energy that stayed with us for around thirty seconds, before it dispersed. Jane and I were completely taken aback by the intensity of the experience, though we agreed it was not at all unpleasant. We continued our tour, though nothing further occurred, and after returning to the kitchen, realised that who ever had been there was no going to come back.

Leaving a questionnaire for a friend of Jane's, I caught the bus, and returned home. A few weeks later I received a reply, which further backed up our experience, though this time however, the events were centred around the kitchen. From the reply it appeared that the there had been a number of 'strange sensations' felt on a particular landing outside the café and that footsteps had been heard in the back corridor, on occasion. Co-incidentally, I was told, a medium had been visiting the museum and on reaching this area, had mentioned to staff that a 'female presence was in the area and that she felt it was connected to the

173

Laird.' I found this interesting, though it would transpire that there appeared to be other spirits, of more humble origin, active in the building, as I was to find out. Some months later I was able to re-visit the lighthouse and had the good fortune to meet a former keeper. During our conversation, he told me of a number of incidents connected to the building and described the following: "A number of years ago, one of our guides was taking a party on a tour of the lighthouse. On reaching the top, and while in the middle of his talk, he noticed one woman turn and leave the group. Slightly perplexed he continued, and on completing the tour ascended the stairs, found the woman was waiting for him at the bottom. Once the visitors had dispersed, she apologised for leaving so abruptly and hoped he did not think her rude. She went on to explain that while he was talking, she noticed a woman standing directly behind him, wearing a dark shawl who was looking at her." The tour guide completely understood, though was taken aback by the revelation, and thought that the description matched that of 'fisher-woman.' The area was further described, as 'having a strange atmosphere at times, with the feeling of being watched, occasionally mentioned,' and it goes without saying that it was with some trepidation that he took his next tour of the lighthouse. I asked him about the cottage where I had felt a presence, in the kitchen. And his reaction was one of genuine interest. Though he had not felt anything himself in that building, a former employee and resident had. He stated that the employee and particularly his wife had often complained about the atmosphere in one of the back bedrooms and in the kitchen, she had 'hated being in that room'. Perhaps he concluded, you had to be particularly sensitive to feel things, but he was aware of their experiences and felt them to be genuine, as they had often mentioned unexplained noises and objects being moved during their stay. He finished off by saying, that he had heard stories connected to most of the buildings on the site, though most of the activities, he concurred, appeared to be subtle, and certainly there had been no 'bad feelings' recorded by staff. His personal theory is that objects hold memories and ties for people as much as building's and perhaps, the various energies find it hard to disconnect from them.

As I was about to leave, he said, that despite not having anything untoward happen to him during his time at the lighthouse, the Wine Tower was a different story. On the odd occasion he had worked there, he described a feeling of being 'watched, and that he didn't like being there on his own.' I thanked him for his time. The Kinnaird Lighthouse museum is a fascinating building and until fairly recently a place of work and literal beacon for the community. It comes as no surprise that the buildings hold many memories for both the living and those who have moved on. The activity in the area varies, and appears to be spread over a number of locations, suggesting a number of different spirits. There is no hard evidence to suggest who these people are, though it is equally possible to be a combination of either the Laird's daughter, fisher folk from a later period, or a former keeper. As many of the former staff moved away, I have been unable to interview any others at great length. The second hand evidence I received was very welcome and was, in my opinion, definitely genuine, from someone who knows the buildings history intimately. Perhaps the best personal evidence was obtained in the kitchen, and I am in no doubt that if both workers and residents had felt the same as I did, then there can be no argument as to its authenticity.

Some short stories

The following stories were recounted to me recently and although I had no personal involvement in them, I felt they were worthy of inclusion due to the wide spectrum of activities witnessed. Hospitals have long been seen as a stomping ground for spirit activity, the reason goes without saying. I was told recently two such tales the first involving a nurse the other a patient. The first took place in ward 4 or latterly the Balgownie ward of the Old Royal Cornhill Hospital in Aberdeen. The hospital opened in the late eighteenth century and was known uncharitably as the Aberdeen Lunatic Hospital. It was described to me as having a reputation amongst staff and being a 'spooky place'. Particularly oppressive were the corridors running between wards one and four and six and seven in which staff didn't tend to linger. Retired nurse, Eileen, worked there for many years and was well aware of the feelings associated with that area. She takes up the story: "Myself and a patient entered the lower corridor washroom and toilet area. I was there to assist my patient with her washing and dressing. There was most definitely no one else present. The vacant/engaged sign on the nearest toilet door started going from vacant to engage at an alarming rate. I pulled the door open and there was no one there. We left the area with great speed and I felt very frightened and shaky." When asked what time of the day this occurred, she replied around, "7.45-8.15 in the morning." Eileen was thankful that this phenomena was never repeated though she was still uncomfortable in certain areas of the building and 'was convinced what I experienced was poltergeist activity'. I have been told many other stories relating to the hospital but as they are either second or third hand I have not included these at the moment. Suffice to say figures have been seen in its many corridors in different locations at the hospital. One common thread is the fact that many of these stories are centred round Elmhill House a former part of the hospital and now luxury housing. Elmhill House was built in 1862 being designed by architect Archibald Simpson. Controversially its recent

176

refurbishment was at the cost of the hospital's 'secret garden' a quiet spot favoured by patients. A building where emotions run high may well retain negative residual energy. It is however, interesting to note that it lay semi derelict for years after a bombing raid which apparently claimed the life of a nurse. Given the nature of hospitals and the duality of life and death it is no surprise that activity is sometimes witnessed in these locations.

The second short story took place at Summerfield House in 1976. A maternity hospital in Summerhill since 1948 it is now the site of National Health Service offices. Community worker Anne was in bed when 'I woke up to see a nun carrying a baby. I tried to sit up and get out of bed to go after her but I couldn't move. Another patient saw my distress and pressed the button to the alarm and a nurse came to help me. The figure of the nun was in profile and abruptly disappeared. She spoke reassuringly to me until I had calmed down and I was able to say what I had seen." The ward sister offered her a cigarette 'with the knowing look of someone who had heard a similar story before.' Anne stated that most of her alarm was caused by the fact she thought someone was taking away a baby. Incidentally opposite the hospital lay a children's home. This home, still in use in the 1960s, was run by nuns and Anne remembers as a youngster that a common threat from parents to local children was 'if you didn't behave you would be sent to live with the nuns'. Moving to the centre of Union Street the following was told to me recently by an employee of Primark and though I have not investigated any further it is still worth inclusion. In June 2007 I had gone along to photograph the interior of the old Trades Hall on Union Street. The hall, built in 1848 was the original meeting place of the Seven Incorporated Trades of Aberdeen. More recently it housed a restaurant for the Littlewoods store but now lay empty and due to its listed status retains many of its original architectural features. I met the assistant manager and was shown to the hall, which is now entered through the store. Left to take photographs I became aware of a presence in the room, which lingered for a number of minutes. The icy sensation that accompanies the arrival of spirit was prevalent and I was happy to notice that on one of my images there was an amazingly bright orb, which appeared to be in flight. After mentioning this to the assistant manager she remarked that a number of staff had for years maintained that they had felt a presence in the building particularly in the basement area. The basement lies within one of the arches that exist under Union Street and have become known as vaults and although sounding mysterious in reality their purpose was for storage. The area in question had been sealed up for health and safety reasons, therefore I was unable to gain access. She went on to explain that rumours had circulated for years about a ghostly piper who had been killed in the vicinity with strange noises reportedly being heard in the lower floors of the building. She unfortunately could not elaborate further though she did say that the stories had existed in the days when Littlewoods owned the store. As there was no more to be gleaned I left and decided to look into the history of the immediate area. It transpired that in close proximity to the current building lay the 'kidnappers house', situated on the Green at the foot of 'Boots staircase' it was eventually demolished in 1916, at that time being over three hundred years old. The house was allegedly where kidnapped children in the 18th century were kept before being shipped abroad as slaves and to mask the sound of their cries a piper was employed. This unsavoury practice was supported by council officials who would turn a blind eye to proceedings and is part and parcel of the infamous 'Indian Peter' story. I passed on the information to the assistant manager and she seemed genuinely surprised, as she knew nothing about the kidnappings. It was intriguing to think that perhaps there was some truth in the stories though not meeting anyone who had first hand experience of this, I cannot in all honesty say. Perhaps it is only an urban myth, a fantasy bandied about for years as a means of unnerving new members of staff. Many buildings have stories attached to them that have been part of the fabric for years so perhaps there is more than a grain of truth to it. All I know was that she seemed genuinely surprised.

The Art Gallery on Schoolhill is apparently visited from time to time by spirit, this incident took place in the McBey room. In conversation it came to light that a number of years ago a member of the gallery staff, John sneaked up on his colleague Dorothy with the express purpose of surprising her by taking her photograph. The picture was taken and amid the following hilarity a strange figure was noticed appearing on the developing image. Directly behind Dorothy the figure of what appeared to be a monk could clearly be seen. They could offer no explanation, as they were alone in the area. To add credence to the story nearby Blackfriars Street was named after an order of friars whose monastery lay roughly where the gallery exists today and records show that the Art Gallery was partially built on their graveyard. It has further been recorded that when being built a number of skeletons were discovered while digging the foundations. Though nothing so obvious has occurred since staff have pointed out that occasionally they have felt they are not alone and there has also been reports of an unexplained shadowy figure though this occurred some time back. Keeping with the council there have been a number of reports concerning a figure being seen in the Town House. Situated at the end of Union Street this grand structure could certainly qualify as to what a haunted building should look like and being over a hundred and fifty years old has definitely had many people through its doors. Unfortunately, very little detail is known, but I have been told by three different council employees that a cleaner saw 'something in the basement a number of years ago and was so terrified they never came back'. A colleague stated that he personally finds the building relaxing to work in though 'some think otherwise and never stay late' I hope one day to be able to contact more witnesses to the above stories and provide a fuller picture as I have found them all intriguing. Perhaps the most interesting one for me follows and again I hope to uncover more factual evidence to back this up, but for now here is a poignant tale connected to the bombing raids on Aberdeen in World War Two.

I met Heather through my work, as part of a group researching the Ashgrove area of the city. Working with the group over a number of weeks the conversation turned to the supernatural and Heather began to recount this story. It transpired that she used to be bothered by frantic knocking at her front door and when she went to look there was no one there. This knocking would follow no set pattern and stop for some time before starting up again. Thinking it was someone playing a practical joke she thought nothing more of it. All was quiet for some time until the knocking restarted. Heather was at the door in seconds and ran into the street to find it deserted. Ill at ease she returned indoors. The knocking though sporadic would occasionally start up again though eventually stopped. It remained a mystery and it was only after a conversation with an elderly neighbour that a possible explanation came to light. Her neighbour now in her eighties recounted how during a particularly destructive bombing raid the Cattofield area was badly damaged. On this particular night many people were killed including an ARP warden who had been banging on the door trying to alert the occupiers of what is now Alice's house. Unfortunately I have not been able to verify this. However if it is true then it would appear at first glance to be a classic case of a tragic event being replayed. I have no reason to disbelieve any of the above accounts; I will leave that choice to you.

Leadside Road is our next destination. This historic road is a shadow of its former self, with many of its original buildings being systematically destroyed in the 1980s, particularly a listed grain mill as well as a number of streets in the vicinity. All that really remains is a huddle of tenements near the top of the road and it is in a top floor flat that the following took place in 1991. Linda, a student nurse at the time, shared this flat with a number of others and despite being less than salubrious the rent was cheap and the location central. She had only been in the property a number of days when she was woken in the early morning by a crushing weight on her body. She lay awake petrified, hardly daring to breath, feeling the weight of the body lying next to and partially on top of her. After what seemed an age the feeling dissipated and as if a spell was broken she got 'dressed quickly and left the room'. Her flatmates were naturally sceptical and were convinced she had been asleep at the time and suffering some type of sleep paralysis but she remained convinced otherwise. To compound her feelings of unease she found herself returning from work on occasion to discover her bags scattered around the room and personal Effects moved despite there being a lock on her door. The atmosphere in the house 'became heavy' and she was convinced that a presence was letting itself be known Finding it hard to confide in others she took to staying at friends until she was sure her flatmates would be at home, making excuses to stay out. Despite this she was approached by an irate downstairs neighbour who asked her to stop thumping on the floor stating that it was so bad his light fitting was seen to sway backwards and forwards. Linda assured the neighbour that it was not her making the noise and questioned her two flatmates who stated in no uncertain terms that they were nearly always out at work and could not have been responsible for the noise. Despite her assurances the noise would periodically start up prompting further complaints. The last straw came when her flatmates stereo was tampered with and rendered useless after its wires were severed. She began suspecting the downstairs neighbour who had begun to make things difficult for her, she could not see how he could have gained access through the heavily locked door in the middle of the night and destroyed the stereo while someone was asleep in the room. Linda was convinced the events were being caused by poltergeist activity rather than any one in the flat and began to look for a new home. The opportunity arose soon after and she gladly packed and left. During our meeting she explained how frustrating it was for her at the time as no one would listen to her fears and put the events down to either a fertile imagination or human intervention. She quickly became a much happier person in her new home and was able to concentrate on her studies though she admitted it took a while to put the incidents of Leadside Road to the back of her mind. I can offer no clue as to why this flat in particular was prone to activity and why no one else in the property seemed aware. Perhaps it was down to the sensitivity of the person involved or the fact that she was the only female in the flat. There were certainly no major events of note that I am aware of in the buildings history that could have caused this other than perhaps a former owner who liked to let themselves be known. I have come across numerous cases like this where a spirit person appears to latch onto one particular person and though frightening at times, generally there is no harm meant other than a need to be recognised to say 'I'm still here'.

Given the sheer volume of sightings, real and possible, I have been unable to include all the stories and snippets of stories I have received. Due in some part to sensitivity, many have had to be omitted, including that of an exorcism in the shire, spirit children in two city locations and a haunted hotel. Others have been left out due to scant facts and problems with access, though in some cases it has been down to lack of time, this I hope to rectify in the near future. Perhaps I may have the opportunity to look more closely at the sighting of an elderly lady, seen reflected in a mirror, by both customer and hairdresser at Kross Cut Hair Design, the old Custom House on Regents Quay, where figures have been seen and loud knocking heard, an illicit burial ground on the outskirts of Aberdeen, where alleged spirits have been seen, or the spirit of a monk, who interacted with a young child. The list is ever growing, so watch this space.

Conclusion

Having spent the last three years visiting numerous locations I have been overwhelmed by the willingness of people to recount their experiences. It has obviously been impossible to verify that every experience recounted was genuinely paranormal but the persons concerned believed them to be and therefore when not personally involved I have accepted them in good faith. Given the nature of paranormal research we can only theorise in many cases who the spirit people are likely to be though I would like to think that an educated guess, given the clues, is sometimes better than none at all. There have been other stories put forward to me throughout my research but given the sensitivity of their particular locations and of the people involved I was asked not to include them. It is sad to say but many people are still genuinely afraid of spirit and for a multitude of reasons and would prefer to ignore the signs hoping they will go away. There is however a greater acceptance of the concept of survival after the physical death though again what form it takes is dictated by religious beliefs. It is a paradox that many accept this survival but not in the form of a 'ghost' able to come back and 'haunt the living'. Perhaps the idea of the vengeful unfeeling spirits as favoured in the Victorian ghost story has played a part in this. As a fan of these classic tales they can be rewarding on many levels but let us not forget they were written for the express purpose of providing vicarious thrills for a society that revelled in its conformity. Victorian literature and art is peppered with works conveying a sense of doomed romanticism, therefore it would be nonsense to suggest that everyone who passes over undergoes a personality change, becomes a figure to be feared, out to drive the unwary insane, a persecutor of the living. It is perhaps this suggestion from the past that has made many people equate spirits with inherent evil; one only has to look at the written word from the bible onwards to see this. Just as in this present life people have complex personalities, most despite our foibles, are essentially decent while some not so. Therefore if you accept that the personality remains when in spirit, that the spirit person is a sentient being then it comes as no surprise that encounters with spirit can be happy, moving, joyful but on the other hand occasionally frightening and depressing. The continuation of life after physical death for me is a given but what is most intriguing to me is what form this life takes, a form that we are just beginning to understand. From the residual energy present in many buildings we are able to experience in a subtle manner the lives of those who went before. The residual energy trapped in these buildings is fascinating and at times can appear more tangible especially after a traumatic incident has occurred, strengthening the imprint. Though these 'replays' are witnessed most frequently it is essentially a recording and therefore cannot interact with us. The experience however can become more interactive in the case of visiting spirits or in the more unusual case of a grounded spirit both whom provide the most tangible evidence and give further proof of sentience. I, like many others believe that a ghost and a spirit person are two entirely different things, with the ghost being most thought of as a non sentient recording from the past while the spirit is seen as the opposite complete with personality. It is important to recognise this as the generic ghost was often thought of as a portent of bad luck when seen which again harks back to more unenlightened times. I would imagine that in many cases witnesses were probably seeing a recording that did not posses the capability to interact never mind change the destiny of anyone unlucky enough to see them. It has become apparent to me through my research just how many people live with spirit in its varying forms and how it is not contained within the parameters of the castle or mansion house. Most houses will have inherent connections to the past and it is perhaps up to us to increase our sensitivities to appreciate and understand this. It would appear that living harmoniously in this life will form a blueprint for future generations that can leave either good or bad energy in the ether. I would suggest that although what will happen in the next life is important perhaps what we do today is more so and in that should consider the Karmic notion of what goes around comes around.

Printed in the United Kingdom
by Lightning Source UK Ltd.
131019UK00001B/202-342/P